today or not today

today or not today

Marcus Towell

Library of Congress Control Number:		2017900139
ISBN:	Hardcover	978-1-5245-9722-1
	Softcover	978-1-5245-9721-4
	eBook	978-1-5245-9720-7

Print information available on the last page.

Rev. date: 01/17/2017

To order additional copies of this book, contact:
Xlibris
800-056-3182
www.Xlibrispublishing.co.uk
Orders@Xlibrispublishing.co.uk
754263

Chapter One

Will saw her first, before she saw them. Gazing out bleary-eyed from the back of the wagon, for he had slept fitfully in it last night, he spotted a vision in the early morning-mist. Galloping at full-pelt along the crest of the ridge, way above their track was a figure, almost ghostlike. Dark cloak flying out behind her the woman rode crouched low over her horse's neck, with her own mane of flame hair trailing her. Then she was gone.

He turned and called back to his friend Fulke travelling in the second cart, 'Gyllom did you see that? Did you see her Fulke?'

A face with slitted eyes appeared through the sheets of the following wagon. He too had dark curly hair, the two youths could have been brothers. 'Shakespeare what is it with you? Can nobody sleep if you don't?'

'But Fulke fellow did you miss her, such a sight, a dream'

'Will lad I was enjoying my own dream until you broke it. What are you talking of anyway?'

'Her, the woman'

'Oh sure it would have to be a woman wouldn't it. Will man you're seventeen years old, you're too young to be so fixed on the lasses'

'She wasn't a lass Fulke, she was a woman, such a woman and I'll never see her again. I feel a poem coming-on Fulke'

'Well get writing lad, write her and forget her, for we have a long day ahead if we're to reach York tonight'

'Where's your romance Gyllom, your imagination?'

'Why sure man you have enough for the both of us and some to spare'.

Talk of York served to bring Will down to earth, for as schoolmasters to Sir Alexander Hoghton, he and Fulke Gyllom were acting as guardians to the group of eight children, not much younger than themselves, that they were escorting over to York from their home at Hoghton Tower in Lancashire. Their mission was twofold for as well as being engaged as tutors to the children of the estate the two youths had been enlisted into Sir Alexander's band of players. Will and Fulke were both to play the roles of women in the group's performances of Mystery Plays at the Spring Fayre.

The boys themselves were still sleeping their dreams, probably of the sights and sounds they would encounter at the fair.

'Where are we Fulke? I need to know'

'By Our Lady Shakespeare we're in the middle of nowhere that's where. Just look at it - nothing'.

Will slumped into silence, but only until they crested the next rise, for there, over to the left in the hazy distance was a castle, or a fort, or some grand mansion 'Fulke we're in fairy-land. Look there's even a castle'

The two youths gazed enrapturedly, each instructing their driver to stop awhile.

Their musing was shattered by the thunder of hooves, followed immediately by a cloud of dust appearing round the bend in the track below them. This oncoming horde ground to a halt, then out of the cloud the woman emerged. Will's jaw dropped. Walking her jet black horse towards their two carts she came alone. Her followers were stilled by a single word from her. It had sounded not English to Will's ear, *maybe French?* he thought.

The mirage walked on, becoming more real. There was something more than elegance; certainly her bottle-green riding habit and matching gold-trimmed cape were of the best quality, dazzling to the two lads, but it was how she carried herself, *almost regal* thought Will, *as graceful as a queen*. The one anomaly was that she was not riding side-saddle but as a man, astride her mount. *That accounts for how fast she was riding* Will realised. He sat frozen as she came even closer, drawing to a stop alongside him. He could have reached out and touched her, had he been less of a statue. Speech was impossible for him, as it was for the now similarly smitten Fulke behind him. Shakespeare was transfixed even moreso by her amber eyes, of such a colour he had never before seen. They were lively, as if delicately dancing over his face as she studied him. Will couldn't return her gaze, his own eyes studied the damp grass, but seconds later the magnets drew him back. Her lips half-smiled and she spoke, in a soft but almost husky voice

'Good morrow sir'. Will nervously nodded an acknowledgement before she continued 'I saw your wagons from the hilltop'. Still paralysed. The scene was revised again as the sound of more horses echoed through the mist, pulling to a halt by the others. The woman did not turn. 'What brings you out at this early hour? I usually have the moor to myself'.

Yes you and your fifteen companions he thought but didn't dare say. His tongue was thawing but as he began to answer her question 'Well my lady we're on...' he was interrupted as an officious-looking

3

man rode out of the group and trotted towards them. This red-haired lady failed to concern herself with the scene behind.

The man shouted from ten yards away. 'Ma'am I have told you about riding away from us'.

Will could not believe this impudence. But her reply was sharp, curtly addressed to this intruder whilst still looking at Will, 'Ma'am? Ma'am! How dare you address me so? Brackenby you will suffer for your insolence'. The rebuked man joined them by Will's wagon. 'Lord Scrope shall hear of this when we return. I still have my title you insolent dog' she snapped.

Will's impressions were confirmed *I knew she was a lady, my title she said. But that accent is so strange, a mixture of French and something else, perhaps Scottish.*

'Forgive me your majesty, I was upset at having to chase you'.

Majesty, the address hit Will like a thunderbolt. He leaped down from the cart and fell to his knees beside her horse, face to the turf. Gyllom, who had caught only snatches of the conversation, thought it best to replicate his friend's behaviour and found himself contemplating a cowpat, without knowing exactly why.

The tableau on this early-morning moor could have been the subject of many a painting of the previous two hundred years.

The beautiful woman spoke softly 'Please get up young fellow'. Then her voice grew hard again as she half-turned to look over her shoulder 'Brackenby we are talking. You will return to your men.'

The man failed to move. 'Your majesty I should remind you of your situation'.

Now she faced him for the first time, her mouth two feet from his face as she spat out 'Allez!'.

Brackenby nodded the most cursory of acknowledgements, hardly the deference that Will would have expected, before wheeling his mount and walking it slowly back to the waiting riders.

'Your majesty?' Will could not conceal the amazement from his voice.

'Oh please young man, later. You were telling me of your mission'

'Your majesty'. Will knew his echo sounded like the mumbling of an idiot, but he felt exactly that. His mind was racing though, *The only majesty is Queen Elizabeth, she must be a foreign visitor, but so far from London.*

His rambling thoughts were halted as she spoke again, but in a soft voice, mellowed to surely a French accent, the scottishness diminished. 'Young man I ask, merely from curiosity, what brings you to this moor'. Then as an afterthought she continued 'I cannot keep calling you fellow or young man, what is your name sir?'

Will made his best attempt at a non-dumb expression, hoping his smile was not imbecilic 'Your majesty I am William Shakespeare of Stratford-upon-Avon'

'A long way from home young William'

'Not really your majesty. I've been away from my family home since I left school last year. I'm retained in Lancashire, near Preston your majesty'

'Oh William, may I call you Will?' While he was contemplating whether he actually had to grant permission she spoke again, 'And Will, please refrain from constantly repeating "your majesty", you may call me Marie'

'Marie?' - the stupidity had returned.

'Yes, for I prefer that to what my countrymen here call me, Mary'.

The clouds cleared from Will's brain at the same time as they left his face. 'Mary Stuart' he timidly suggested.

'The very same' she smiled.

'Queen of Scotland, Queen of France' - it was meant as a confirmation but still sounded questioning. A pause while the information sank in, during which time the tousle-haired Fulke joined them. The two youths were now two young boys gazing up at a monarch.

Fulke seemed more capable of rational speech but he kept his voice low as he muttered, just loud enough for Mary to hear 'And some say Queen of England'

Mary shot a glance at the newcomer 'Young man watch your words. Some of that group would hang you up for such a comment' and she tossed her head behind her

Fulke looked rebuked but Mary instantly relieved him, 'Why lads before you tell me what you are about would you kindly tell me exactly who retains you?'

'Your majesty - Marie', Will forced out his amendment, 'We come from Hoghton Tower'.

Mary's face seemed to lighten. She broke into a full smile, 'Sir Alexander Hoghton'

'The same your majesty' Fulke answered.

'Then I believe lads you are of the same faith as myself?'

Will and Fulke glanced anxiously at each other. Despite all of their employer's advice when setting out on their journey, the imploring to never discuss religion with anyone they should meet, they surely could confide in Mary Stuart, the pre-eminent Roman Catholic in Britain. It was Will who answered, 'We are indeed so'. Then he was dumbstruck again by the queen's action. She offered her gloved hand for him to kiss. He pulled himself to and responded to the gesture, noticing as he did so the strange quality of the band of skin between her glove and the wristband of her sleeve -it had a marble-like glow to it. Fulke nervously stepped forward and put his mouth to Mary's glove. The royal beauty turned to look back at her retinue then looked at Will.

'Good sirs if we remain here talking in this damp we'll catch our death of cold. Does your mission allow a diversion?'

Will was determined to comply so he managed a mumbled 'Marie' before informing her 'We have to drive to York your majesty. We carry eight children of the estate and are on our way to the Spring Fayre'.

'And we are expected on Thursday your majesty to perform our Mystery Play' added Fulke

'But boys we are but at Monday, can you not accept a queen's hospitality?'

Now they were confused, for both had known that Mary Stuart was being held a prisoner somewhere in the north of England, but nobody knew where, not even Sir Alexander. How could an imprisoned monarch offer hospitality.

Mary saw how Will was puzzling over her invitation, 'Young Will do not look so worried. Do you know of my situation?'

'I know my lady that you are no longer free'

'Freedom is relative fine fellow. I have my captors' and she lowered her honey-like voice, 'But you should know that my guardian Lord Harry Scrope is not a heretic but one of us'. Will and Fulke became two open-mouthed country bumpkins. Mary continued 'Certainly I am bound to remain at Bolton Castle, which you see across the valley. But as you see I am not yet bound in chains'

Will and Fulke simultaneously considered a nervous smile to be appropriate. Younger faces were now peering out of each of the wagons, each displaying varying degrees of puzzlement. The two youths stared at each other, then Will took up the conversation 'Hospitality your majesty?'

'Yes Will I would that you all join me for some hours at Castle Bolton where we can talk in what passes for comfort'

Will felt it to be quite brazen but he said it nevertheless 'Marie who are we to refuse a royal command?'

Her laugh was loud and long and provoked exchanges of frowns amongst the distant gathering. 'Then Will I will command two of my own men, not Brackenby's rabble, to escort you down to my castle. I must ride some more but will meet you there.'.

Will smiled inwardly at her attitude *She really does consider it to be her castle.*

With a gentle lowering of her head to the right their regal acquaintance turned her horse, trotted it back to the group then as she reached them she urged her animal into a canter straight past them. The pack of hounds set off in chase again.

Will and Fulke turned and grabbed each other, laughing furiously. 'Fulke man that puts the poem on hold what? She's real and we know her' and Will clapped his friend on the back as he gave out a yell that bounced back off the hillside.

A babble of young voices increased in volume 'William, Fulke, what's happening?' called out young Richard Appleby, a thirteen year-old whose rosy face reflected his surname.

'Boys how do you fancy a day in a castle with a real queen?'

'Don't tease us sir' pleaded the over-sensible Jamie Duberry, a thin lad of twelve going-on eighteen.

'Lads I'd not do that. Do you know who that lady was, any of you?'

'Please sir I did hear you call her your majesty, why was that sir?'

'Because Frederick, because that elegant, beautiful, and friendly woman was....' He had the attention of sixteen eyes and ears, 'She was....The Queen!' he yelled, without any specification of whom she ruled.

'Please sir, I don't think so. Queen Elizabeth lives in London' corrected Richard.

'No Richard, our queen. What is your religion young Dick?'

'Sir you know we mustn't tell anyone that'. Will admired the boy for his obedience to Sir Alexander's ruling, even though he had disobeyed it himself.

'Come here lads, down from the carts'. His audience gathered and waited. 'This is a secret, probably the most important you have ever shared. That lady my fine lads was Mary Queen of Scots' A communal intake of breath was the only response. A shout was heard from Mary's pair of riders and Will turned to them 'We're on our way sirs. Come on lads back in the wagons and off to the castle'

Only one voice of reason rang out – the Duberry boy again 'But sir what about the fair?'

'There's time enough for that tomorrow lads. Today we dine with royalty'.

Chapter Two

Sam saw her first before she saw him. The young woman was halfway up the escarpment to his right, looking through binoculars, over his head, at the castle at the top of the long incline to his left. It had been a tough trek for him across the moor from Hawes. He turned back to continue his walk along the road leading to the village of Castle Bolton, when suddenly there was a frightened yell from the girl and he looked back to see her slipping down the loose stones of the hillside towards the ditch running alongside the road. Sam sprinted back as her own speed gathered momentum, out of control. Sam leapt across the narrow dyke and braced himself in her line of flight. She was screaming frantically then looked up to see the man watching her.

'Oh shit! Out of the way' she yelled. 'Mind out you fool'. She was nearly at him as he spread out his arms and moved towards her. Crunch - the collision happened. Entwined together they rolled over and over down the remaining few yards to the bottom. The girl lay there shaking and panting as Sam recovered his breath. She suddenly appreciated the work of her saviour 'Oh sir thank you, thank you. I thought I was in for a big one. Shit what happened?'

'I think lass that you were more intent on the view than your footing, yea?'

The girl was flushed as she offered her hand, 'I'm Kate Courtney. Thank you again'

Sam smiled back at her 'Sir Galahad, mountain rescue division'

Kate smirked. 'So there are still knights in that castle then'.

Sam appreciated her counter. 'Ok I lied, but I'm glad I was here. Sam Woodhouse'

'Oh Sam so am I believe me' she gasped.

He studied this girl as she dusted herself down, tallish, slim and with that stunning combination of brown eyes and blonde hair, cut into a neat bob. He guessed her age to be early twenties. As she continued her tidying she spoke without looking at him 'It's a lonely spot here, I was lucky there was somebody around. Hell I could have ended up lying injured in that ditch for hours or more, or worse'

'Best not to dwell on what might have been, bit of a belief of mine'

Kate now looked more closely at this guy who spoke in staccato sentences. He was slightly taller than her, sympathetic green eyes, fair hair cut in a spiky style. *I reckon he must be late thirties* she estimated.

'Kate, right, yes? Kate can I ask what you were doing up there - bit of a dodgy spot'

'Well I'm hiking, a sort of working holiday trip, and I always prefer to get off the beaten track a bit. I'd walked over that hill from Leyburn then I turned off the footpath onto Redmire Moor. I saw this road and tried to take a shortcut down'

'Kate I'm a walker too but if there's a simple route I usually take it'

She laughed 'Guess that's why the other students call me Crazy Kate'

Students? thought Sam *She must be even younger than I thought.* 'You're a student?' he asked.

'Yes I'm at Lancaster Uni, doing my Ph.D.'

Ah a permanent student Sam concluded, *probably is about twenty-three or four then.* 'You said a working trip' he asked.

'Yes I'm on my way to Bolton Castle up there' and she waved an arm up the opposite hillside.

'Snap'

'Yes?'

'Look Kate it's about lunchtime, I was going to have a spot to eat. Must be a pub in the village. Care to join me?'

'Well I certainly need a brandy or something, I'm still a bit shaky' the girl replied.

'Are you O.K. to walk'

Kate bent her jean-clad legs and flexed her ankles 'Yes sure. Anyway I don't see too many taxis around, or are you offering to carry me?"

Sam smiled as he thought, *A forthright northern lass alright*, for he had already placed her Mancunian accent.

'I'll race you there' Kate joked as she mocked a sprint start

'Think you've done enough running young lady'

'Lady, that's quaint' she teased him.

Sam grinned and offered his arm but she declined in a friendly manner, her eyes creasing into a smile 'I'm ok Sam, honestly, but thanks for offering'.

They wandered up the narrow lane, between high hedges, and turned into the village of Castle Bolton where they reached the imposing castle, its miserable dark brown stone walls towering gauntly against the sky; not as romantic as it had seemed from a distance.

'Surely looks impregnable' Sam remarked 'A good place for a prison'. Kate turned to him without speaking, but wondering why he had mentioned a prison. They reached the pub, each stooping to enter through the old oak doorway. 'Brandy yes?'. Kate nodded.

Sam returned with their drinks, a double for Kate, and two menus. 'There's also the blackboard'

'No thanks the chalk gets in my teeth' she laughed, prompting Sam to smilingly frown at her.

'Right madam, I'm starting to get your humour. So for sweet I'm going to have apple rollover and over and over'. Kate slapped his golden arm.

Two steaming steak and ale pies arrived, appreciated by both. Neither spoke as they ate, perhaps sizing up their newly-met companion.

Kate broke the silence as they sat back 'Having a pud? But don't you dare order the turnover or I'm walking out of here!' she laughed.

'Can't really eat a sweet, too full.'

'We could share a sticky-toffee pudding'

'Alright you've tempted me' Sam agreed.

Now sated they sat back to enjoy their second drinks. Sam spoke first 'You said a working holiday. D'you mean you're a historian? No that would be too much of a coincidence'

Kate looked puzzled, 'No I'm not, but sort of related. Anyway why a coincidence? Is that what you are Sam?'

'Yes. I write a bit. Nothing on at the moment but I've come here because of my favourite person from history. But what are you studying Kate?'

'Who is this fav person? I'm intrigued now'

'I asked first' said Sam in a mock schoolboy taunt

Kate was enjoying this guy's company. 'I'm a literature student - Shakespeare'. She looked for a bored reaction implying 'not another one. How much more can there be on that guy?' but Sam's eyes gave no hint of such a response. Instead his question was positive

'Well from what I've learnt of you already Kate I reckon you've got a different angle on him'

Kate felt sure she was blushing, but he would think it is the brandies, *Anyway I don't blush.* 'Well' she paused, 'You see there's this theory that Shakespeare was actually a Roman Catholic in his youth, that his father was what we call a Recusant, a closet Catholic so to speak, and that he brought up his family likewise. I went to a conference run by the uni on this last year and there's a growing belief in it. My studies are investigating catholic allusions in his texts. Sorry that must sound boring'

'You're joking! It's incredible, I'm hooked. 'Cause isn't there some doubt about where he was and what he did after he left school in Stratford?'

'Exactly, his 'Lost Years' they call them. From when he was sixteen until he turned up in London when he was twenty-eight. We know he got married and had three children, but there's no proof that he hung around Stratford. There's increasing evidence that he came up north, to teach near Preston. Look this is all a bit heavy, tell me who your historical hero is'

'No Kate I'm really interested'

'Well let's talk about it later. Now, I have to guess. You said he's connected to this castle?'

'She'

'Ah, you mentioned it being a prison. I know - Mary Queen of Scots'

'Brilliant'

'Not at all, she's from the same period that I'm studying isn't she?'

'Yes, a bit older than your Bard but she was around'

Kate was excited 'Hey Sam it is a coincidence then. We're both into Tudor times'

'Why yes young mistress Kate, but I prithee thou art no shrew'

Kate's laughter was loud, impulsive and genuine, no polite affectation. It caused the other three heads in the bar to turn around.

They finished their drinks and headed back up the lane to the castle.

Chapter Three

The carts rumbled up the narrow rutted track to the village of Castle Bolton and pulled up outside the imposing castle. There was no sign of their royal acquaintance, nor of anyone else.

The sun broke through and cleared the mist.

'Will do you think we dreamed we'd met Queen Mary, for there's no sign of her? Shall I go and bang on the gates?'

'Patience Fulke, we've only just arrived. Anyway a queen is allowed to keep people waiting'

Fulke raised his eyebrows to mock Shakespeare. His voice was full of doubt as he asked 'Will are you sure we are not being stupid? You know we have to prepare the play, and the others will be expecting us in York'

'Fulke man they left on Saturday, they'll be setting up the stage and having rehearsals. If we are a day late so what. Do you not remember that we lost a wheel from your wagon and it took us almost a day to repair it?' he smiled.

'We did? Jesus Shakespeare you're a wicked one'

Shortly afterwards the clatter of hooves was heard, announcing the royal entourage. Mary trotted on when she saw her newly-met sympathisers. 'Have you been here long lads? I had to give a good exercise to my black beauty here for yesterday I could not ride, I was under treatment from my physician, Mr. Burson. One gets all kinds of chills in this bleak place. It's not like the Loire Valley, for I was never cold at Chambord'

'No your majesty... Marie, we arrived but minutes ago'

Mary looked about her impatiently, 'Why do they not open the gates? Somebody must have seen our approach. For heaven's sake it's their wish that I return here, for surely with this horse I could leave them anytime I wish. In fact young sirs my keeper, Sir Francis Knowles, has written to Elizabeth to that effect, and...,' she lowered her voice '...I hear it from Mr. Nawe, my secretary, that Knowles has even suggested to the Virgin that it might be better to let me escape. The problem is where would I go, for at this time my Scotland is dominated by my brother and those treacherous rebel lords, but more of that another time. Come lads lets warm ourselves with mulled wine. When those wretches decide to let us enter'. She turned back to Brackenby and yelled like a man. 'Do they not want me back? Get these doors open'. As she spoke the heavy doors swung apart. 'Bring your carts into the yard Will, you can't trust these English village folk'. She smiled, 'Why sir I do forget you are so yourselves'. Will smiled, thinking this must be the closest a monarch would get to an apology.

The party clattered through into the cobbled courtyard, followed by Will and Fulke's wagons. The youngsters spilled out of them and gazed up in awe at the towering castle, five storeys high. A portly-looking man walked towards Mary as she came to speak with Will. 'Your majesty, Burson has been fretting. He claims you were advised not to ride today'

Mary ignored this information, her response was to introduce her young companions 'Will, and...' she paused.

'Fulke Gyllom your majesty'

'Boys this is Mr. Curle, my Master of Horse. Curle, my friends William Shakespeare and Fulke Gyllom'

'Friends?' thought Will 'Would it were so!'

Curle nodded to the pair. He presented a comical figure with his legs widely bowed

'Your sister Curle, is feeling better? She too suffers from these climes' Mary explained to the lads.

'Thank you ma'am yes'.

She began to stride across the courtyard to the tower in the far left corner and without turning called back 'Mr. Curle tell Mrs. Bastion to bring breakfast for eleven hungry mouths to The Solar. And mulled wine for Will, Fulke and myself, two jugs sir'.

'Sir, sir what's happening? Why are we here?' called young Thomas Croft, a lad who constantly wore an expression of bemusement.

Will turned back and lifted the worried little face level with his own, 'Tom lad you are going to eat with a queen, that's what. When you are an old man you can tell your grandchildren of this morning. I'll warrant they won't believe you, but you'll have this memory lad'

A high-pitched cheer rose from the gaggle as they ran to catch up with Mary. She turned and smiled softly at Will for she had heard every word of his explanation to the boy. Will caught her glance and the effect was a jab of excitement. He turned to his friend 'Poetry couldn't write this moment Fulke', then muttered 'This is no Warwickshire wench man. Just look at her. And that voice'

'Steady Shakespeare'

'Fulke what is it they say? A cat may look at a queen'

'Yes Shakespeare but she shouldn't hear him purring!'

Will slapped his friend's shoulder. 'Come boy, we've wine to sip' and he ran ahead.

The two teachers had almost completed the climb up two flights of stairs and were approaching the Solar when they realised that their group of pupils had shrunk to only three. They rapidly retraced their steps and found two lads in the Malting House on the first floor, then a floor below the remainder were fascinatedly watching a wretched-looking bay horse walking wearily round in circles - the Horse Mill. Six little eyes were peering through the sweet-smelling dust at this ancient scene.

'Richard, Guy, Samuel come on quickly. Do you not want breakfast?'. The heads reluctantly turned silently away and followed Will back upstairs.

Queen Mary was in the Solar talking with two of her servants, an elderly man and a young woman about Will's age. 'Now she is more my taste' said Fulke leeringly. Will kicked his ankle.

'Behave knave'

'Always the poet eh Will' Gyllom mocked.

Mary came across to them. 'Now what are you two whispering about?' The remark was directed at Will who reddened, partly at the need to conceal the topic of their banter but moreso at the smirking sexy expression on the monarch's face.

'Just idle talk, of no consequence' he managed to stammer.

Cheeky Sam Baker earned himself a cuff on one of his stick-out ears from Fulke as he pointed at him and proclaimed 'Your majesty, I heard them. Mr Gyllom has taken a fancy to your maidservant'

Mary was unsmiling as she addressed the boy, 'Young man someone should teach you never to tell tales. It can be very dangerous'. Baker dropped his head and skulked off. Mary turned to Shakespeare 'And what of your fancy Will. Is there some young damsel missing you back at Hoghton?'.

'No my lady'. He boldly decided to look her in the eye as he answered, perhaps already searching for any reaction to his words.

Mary's tone changed as her voice again was lowered, 'I would talk with you of less frivolous matters after we have taken breakfast. Come.' The party walked to the table, which had hastily been prepared beneath the south-facing windows. It was festooned with cold meats, fresh bread, fruit and pies. The boys' eyes bulged, such a spread they usually saw only at lunchtime or dinner, even those who lived in the main house at Hoghton. A jug of wine was carried to the table from its warming niche behind the grand fireplace. Will walked off alone and was gazing out of the adjacent window when Mary joined him, carrying two glasses of spicy mulled wine. 'I cannot complain of the views they have provided' she smiled. 'It isn't Scotland but yonder Penn Hill has a charm. Do you recognise it Will?'

'No Marie, are you sure I am correct to use your name your majesty?'

'Would you rather I called you Mister Shakespeare?' she rejoined.

Will grinned, containing his delight at this woman's affirmation of friendship. 'No Marie, I have never been in these parts before' he eventually responded to her question.

'I think you know that place though sir, it's where a young schoolteacher once met a Scottish queen'. This time Will's youth betrayed him with a blush. Mary continued 'I spend a lot of my day writing letters in here, attempts to seek release from this unjustified situation in which I find myself. I have sought assistance from France, appealing to the Duke of Anjou and the Cardinal of

Lorraine, even Catherine de Medici; all to no avail. I fear they do not wish to believe in my innocence in the matter of that wretch Darnley. I fled my prison on Loch Leven, helped by the way by a lad no older than you, then came to England to gain refuge with Elizabeth, my cousin queen, and instead I now find myself imprisoned again. Would you credit it? - even my own brother Moray sided with the English Queen against me! William I believe Lancashire to be a county where attitudes to my religion are less condemning. Would I be right?'

Will felt an elation and a pride that this monarch should discuss such serious matters with him, but knew that he must remain ever cautious. 'I have to say ma'am that in our infrequent travels within the county we meet mostly Catholics but open declarations or practice of Catholicism are never made. We are all recusant in these troubled times, for there are as you know many treacherous ears abroad'

Mary took his arm, 'Will we will talk anon. Let us join your fellows'. Her manner lightened as she led him back to the table and turned to the youngsters. 'Boys are you familiar with the sport of football?'

Richard, the eldest and therefore most confident replied, 'Your majesty we have a cloth ball at Hoghton, but it is a poor game we play'

'Well lads when I first came to England I was forced to reside in Carlisle Castle and many an afternoon I would stroll to the green and watch a game of football. My stable grooms have a pigskin ball and you may take that across to the village green outside the gates. You may find the local boys will join you, but you will be Queen Mary's team.'. A great cheer rang up, causing the three ladies-in-waiting to rush to the doorway from their quarters in the small room off the Solar.

The mood changed as if by a switch when a heavily-built frowning man brushed through the far doorway. His bushy eyebrows and gloomy countenance sent a chill through young Will. Mary turned to confront him, feigning politeness 'Why Sir Francis how can I help you?'

The newcomer was not happy 'Your majesty I am informed you are entertaining unauthorised visitors. Is this true?'

'Knowles do you not see them? William, Fulke, this is my keeper Sir Francis Knowles, he together with Lord Henry Scrope whose home we share'. She turned back to her warden 'Why Knowles do you say unauthorised? I need no permission to receive whatever guests I so desire. Or are further restrictions now imposed?' With which she turned to Will 'Come Master Shakespeare, we must find fresher air than here'. Knowles brusquely about-turned and swept out. Mary turned to them all and shrugged whilst smiling, then called out 'Mrs. Mowbraye, a football by the gates, and Mrs. Pearpoint my cape if you please'. Will was staggered, impressed by the supreme confidence and authority of this beautiful woman that all of England knew was being held a prisoner somewhere; but a prisoner she did not seem.

As the excited group left the castle Will found himself walking alone with Mary; she whispered to him 'Knowles's bark is worse than his bite, I hear he has a certain concealed fondness for me and has in fact sung my praises as a woman to Elizabeth. She was apparently furious with him when he spoke of my elegant tongue and my stout courage'. This incongruous pair, a middle-aged monarch and a callow youth, exchanged muted smiles, Will not quite managing to conceal how dazzled he was by this sparkling woman.

Mary, two yeomen of her warder and Will and Fulke were spectators on the green, watching as the Hoghton boys were immediately joined by a gaggle of ill-dressed youths from the village, whose generally larger size and rough play caused a succession of cuts and bruises: the queen's team eventually capitulating, to the jeers of the village ruffians.

On the walk back to the castle Mary took Will to one side. 'Will, I am enjoying the company of people who are neither servants nor jailers. Can I implore you to stay this evening? I would dearly love to have you give some recitation or performance for me'

Will now felt it perhaps time to practice what he had always been advised to do but rarely did, to make his head over-rule his heart. But he did not wish to seem the maker of such a decision and therefore replied 'Marie I must first speak with Fulke for we share a responsibility'

'Of course'.

Two minutes later he returned and, looking dejected, spoke 'My lady we feel we will be placed in serious trouble should we not make our way to York, for we are expected tonight but now it will already be late tomorrow morning before we arrive'

Queen Mary looked truly disappointed. 'Will can you make me a promise?'. His face showed her that he would cross the world for her. 'Would you and all of your company of players come here on your return journey to perform some part of your play? A feast shall be prepared for you. I will order accommodation to be set up in the courtyard. When do you return? Is it agreed?'

Will lifted his shoulders and smiled broadly, answering both questions. 'Your majesty we return on Sunday next and I will tempt my senior players with an offer to attend a royal banquet'.

Now Mary's face lit up. 'I shall wait the six days'. She grinned before adding 'But you do realise that to break a promise to a queen is treason'. Will's smile was more nervous.

Upon their re-entry into the castle the teachers and pupils were given a tour of it by their hostess, who to all intents was acting as the actual owner. Mary then summoned her surgeon to tend the boys' injuries and she sent to the kitchens for provisions to be made up. It seemed to Will that the quantities that were placed in their wagons would feed an army for a week.

'Well Will you have to eat tonight and enjoy a hearty breakfast tomorrow morning before you complete your journey to York. But you will take lunch with me yes'. Will realised that this was not really a question, it was a command, one which he readily persuaded Fulke to agree to.

The party, each of whom had eaten more in four hours than they had in the past three weeks, went towards the stairs down to the courtyard, with heavy heels to match their stomachs, for they would willingly have remained here - better a royal castle than tents on the outskirts of York. Mary drew Will back as the others were leaving. 'Would a handsome fellow grant a queen a kiss of farewell?' and she put her cheek out for him, taking his hands and squeezing them as he complied, in the French manner, tentatively brushing each cheek in turn. She looked into his face, 'My men will accompany you to

Leyburn. I believe you will then be on your original route yes? I shall wave from this window. Au revoir mon beau William'

'Au revoir Marie'

A brief exchange of impassive gazes then Will turned and danced down the stone steps to the courtyard and leaped onto the cart in one bound, crying out joyfully 'Come lads, on to York'.

Chapter Four

Sam and Kate wandered slowly back up the lane from the pub to the castle, pausing to watch the local children enjoying a kick-about game of football on the village green fronting the row of ancient cottages. There was one player, more skilled than the others, who caught their attention, a tallish gangly player, a flame-haired girl.

'Look at her!' said Kate enthusiastically 'she could get a place in my team anytime'

'You like footy then?' asked Sam, trying to keep the sexist surprise out of his voice.

'You're joking. I play for the uni women's team and I never miss a match at Preston North End. I go with two of the lads from Postgrad College'

'Ah Kate, I thought you a woman of taste...but Preston?' he taunted. 'I've got a season ticket for Middlesbrough'.

'Middlesbrough eh! F.A. Cup sixth-round 1925. Preston 2 - Boro 1?'

'Ooh!. I see your research doesn't only cover Mr. Shakespeare madam'

Kate smiled, warming more to this guy. 'I suppose you went to that match did you?' and she had to laughingly skip away to avoid his threatened slap. 'No! no! But why Middlesbrough? Is that where you live Sam?'

'No, I live not that far from here, Barnard Castle, north of Richmond'.

They arrived at the archway of the castle entrance and bought tickets from the booth inside on the left, Sam also taking a guidebook. The elderly ticket-seller was pleasant and on Sam's referring to Mary Queen of Scots she informed them that only one of the four original towers remained intact and luckily that was the South-West one, containing what had been Mary's apartments.

Kate and Sam first explored the ruins of the guardroom and the bakery and brew-house before passing through a doorway and looking in on the site of the old Horse-Mill, imagining some poor creature spending its days in a perpetual circle. They climbed up stone steps to the malting-house and granary before continuing to a landing where they found a souvenir-shop on the right and the roofless chapel through a door to the left. They walked through to the far end of the chapel to inspect the tiny Priest's Cell. Returning in silence to the landing they mounted the few steps up to the Solar, a room which was now cheered by the rays beaming through the leaded windows.

'Oh Sam what a view!' exclaimed Kate 'Come and look'. The pair of them gazed out onto the rolling countryside. 'That must be the hill where we met'

'You mean where you fell for me?' laughed Sam, pleased with his own pun, but Kate was not smiling. Then, after glancing behind, he opened one of the windows.

'Sam should you do that?'

'I just want to make a gesture, for I would certainly have helped Mary to escape if I had been around'.

A throat-clearing from behind spun them both round. 'Not far from the truth young man. I'm Harry Orde-Powlett'. A pink-faced lightly-built man was smiling at them.

'Is this your place then?' asked Sam, a little flippantly.

'Yes it is actually. But you were talking of escape and did you know that my ancestor, the ninth Baron Scrope, another Harry, even wrote to London suggesting that Mary be permitted to get away from Bolton Castle. He proposed that perhaps a rope of bedsheets might be used'

'No?' queried Kate

'Yes young lady. For they saw her imprisonment here as something of an embarrassment. Sir Henry was a Roman Catholic you know, his wife was the sister of the Duke of Norfolk, but Elizabeth considered that this would somehow place him beyond suspicion of aiding Mary unlawfully. Strange logic. I heard your comment sir. I gather you have sympathy for the Scottish Queen'.

'Well she's always fascinated me - tragic heroine and all that' Sam answered.

'Of course. Well if you want any more information on her time here we have a website which you and your girlfriend should look at'. Sam and Kate looked a little sheepishly at each other. 'Oh I'm sorry, have I been presumptive?'

'No no, that's alright' assured Kate. 'We're just friends'

'Have been for three hours' laughed Sam

'Well its been nice meeting you both. Don't forget to shut the window will you', with which the Honourable Harry smiled and left.

Sam turned to Kate 'Oops, red-face time'

'Because of what? The window or his mistake about us?'

'Oh the window' Sam grinned, reaching for it.

'That's alright then' Kate nudged him. Then she walked across the room, 'Look Sam what do you think this little cubby-hole is by the fireplace?'

'To warm something up maybe. Could be the wine, you know mulled wine'

'Of course. I love that in the winter don't you?'

'Never tried it'

'Oh you must. I'll make some when we....when we have some cold weather, I expect. I usually do' Kate said, quickly amending her sentence.

Since it was a Monday afternoon there were no other visitors therefore Sam and Kate had the castle to themselves as they slowly wandered round the apartments.

'Isn't this great Sam, with no-one else around you can just imagine we are back then'

'Mmm' acknowledged Sam. He had long been looking forward to this visit to Bolton Castle but now that he was here he found he could give it less than full attention, for his preoccupation was diluted by his new companion, an unplanned diversion.

'Sam. You O.K.?'

'Of course Kate. I was just thinking how good it is to share this visit with someone'

Kate's smiling acknowledgement tingled his neck, a sensation which spread on hearing her reply 'For me too Sam'.

They went upstairs to the former Bed Chambers of Lord and Lady Scrope. In the latter there was a magnificent dark-wood four-poster bed with intricate carving on it. 'Look at that Kate, I love those beds. My grandmother had one when I was a kid'

'Ah but that was when they were new wasn't it?' Sam liked the way she teased him about their age-difference but it did not seem to stop them getting on well together. 'Sorry Sam, there's not that much between us. You know I'm joking'

'That's alright my dear, but can you just help me up these steps - age you know'. Kate's slap was fun-filled.

They walked across to what had been the Lord Scrope's bedchamber, which had been used by Mary as her private living room. Sam revelled in the fact that apparently they were walking on the original floorboards, literally following in his heroine's footsteps, but he was brought back to reality by the sight of the various waxwork tableaux provided for tourist consumption. He turned to Kate 'Shall we go the whole way and climb up onto the roof, it says there's a way up there'

'Of course. I want to try everything'

They found the spiral staircase but the last leg of the ascent necessitated the negotiation of a steep stepladder up to the battlements. Sam played the gentleman, standing at the foot of the steps lest Kate should slip, but this was not entirely good manners for it required him to contemplate an ascending bottom clad in tight-fitting jeans. He then went up and joined Kate on the roof.

'Wow Sam just look at it! Well worth the effort. And look the at steepness of that slope, I must have been crazy to try and walk down there'

'Well worth the effort though' he smiled. A remark which prompted Kate to actually link her arm through his and squeeze it. After standing like this for several moments in the summer breeze, Sam spoke 'How about a good old-fashioned English tea?'

'Sounds great, come on. Oh God we've got those steps to get down'

Sam went first then took Kate's hand to help her. He was surprised by the soft feminine feel of her skin. It had been two years since the split with Sally and he had forgotten how good it was to touch. Three steps from the bottom Kate stopped. Sam looked up at her questioningly, 'Bet you can't catch me again' she squealed as she launched herself towards him.

They clung together laughing. 'Woman if you're going to make a habit of that can you give me more warning next time' Sam spluttered.

They found the Guest Hall, which was still a place to dine, but the menu comprised only cream scones and afternoon tea in this century. They sat at a corner-table despite the absence of other occupants. Their mood had changed a little now, perhaps sensing that the time of departure, and hence the closure of their transitory friendship, was approaching. Sam felt a slight sickness in the pit of his stomach. It had been what he called 'a megaday'. But the question had to be asked, 'How far were you planning on getting today Kate?'

She looked at her watch 'Shit Sam its nearly five. I had planned to reach Hawes tonight, but there's no way...'

'No there isn't. I know because I came over from there this morning, you'll never make it before dark'.

They looked at each other concernedly, then Sam spoke 'Look Kate I have an idea. If you don't like it I'll understand. I'm on the last day of my holiday, I've been walking over from Lake Windermere. I've only walked one way, I caught a train and busses to Bowness from Leyburn, where you were this morning. I drove there from Barnie and I've left my car at the railway station.' Kate's expression was blank, awaiting his next words. 'I planned to reach there tonight and drive home but what if we both go to Leyburn now, then we could relax, have dinner, book a couple of rooms in a hotel and in the morning I'll drive you over to Hawes before I head for home. What do you think? Say no if you think it's stupid. Otherwise I could drive you from Leyburn to Hawes tonight but….' And his voice faded out as Kate gazed into his eyes. Sam looked for further clues in her expression but it displayed neither delight nor dismay at his proposal, but perhaps a slight dimpling at the corners of her mouth, a pleased resignation?

She answered slowly and softly 'Sam…'. He braced himself. 'Look I'm going to be very honest, at the risk of making a fool of myself. I have really really enjoyed today. I don't want it to end. I….' Kate put her hand over his on the table. Then she leant across and whispered, despite the lack of company 'Can I take the Hawes in the morning option? You're sure you don't mind Sam, being lumbered with me?'

Sam gave her a tender smile, 'Well somebody has to make sure an old man doesn't lose his way to Leyburn and you know the route, but no mountainsides O.K.?'

Kate jumped up and kissed him on both cheeks then happily skipped to the cash desk and paid while Sam was still getting the strength back in his trembling legs.

Chapter Five

The five miles to Leyburn were travelled by Will with his head in the clouds but he was grounded when Mary's two men pulled their horses up alongside his cart. 'Well young sir we must leave you now, we wish you God speed'

'Thank you fellows, we will see you again on Sunday' he called out joyfully. The two men looked at each other in puzzlement, shrugged their shoulders then wheeled their mounts and set off back to Castle Bolton.

Fulke had heard Will's words to the yeomen from his wagon behind and he yelled out to his companion 'Shakespeare what was that you said about Sunday?'

'I'll tell you when we stop' and he flapped the reins to urge his carthorse forward.

The miles seemed to pass slowly for Will, each one taking him further away from his new-found happiness.

The sky turned pink and half an hour later the little wagon train was approaching Ripon. Will called back to Fulke, indicating that they should stop for the night. He climbed through into the back of the cart and found the four boys there already searching through the mountain of foodstuff which Mary had provided for them. 'Lads, lads, come on. This fine spread merits a proper picnic. Thomas, you and Samuel lay out two blankets on the ground. David and Rich stand behind the cart and I'll pass you out what we'll eat tonight'. Will found even a huge bottle of wine had been included and was surprised to see that Fulke had his own independent stock of provisions. The two groups joined for their impromptu party then, with stomachs full, the eight boys ran to a patch of green and produced a football. 'How have you come by that?' asked a surprised Will.

'Sir Mrs. Mowbraye gave it to us. She said Queen Mary told her it was a gift from her and we should keep it'. Will felt a thrill just hearing that name spoken.

Left alone the two teachers looked at each other. Will knew what was coming, 'Shakespeare'

'Mmm'

'Never mind mmm. What of Sunday? Why should you tell the yeomen we will see them on Sunday?'

Shakespeare had an idiotic grin on his face. 'Fulke fine fellow, we have received a royal command. I am to tell the other players that our journey home must pass through Castle Bolton'

'And why might that be Shakespeare?'

'Why sir we are asked to perform our play before a queen'

'No! You're teasing Will'

'Fulke there is to be a fine banquet, accommodation for the night. Would you have refused?'

'William I feel it was not the prospect of fine food which prompted your acceptance'

'Why what else lad? Come fine fellow lets show these saplings how to play football' and away he ran. Fulke just sat on the ground, he too now wearing a wide grin.

The following morning Will woke everybody at dawn. After a huge breakfast the boys all climbed back into the wagons to return to sleep while Will and Fulke drove on, anxious that their arrival be as little delayed as possible, to mitigate the scorn of their fellows waiting in York.

The boys had been sworn to secrecy about the diversion, having been told to support the invented tale of a broken wheel, but Shakespeare now had to tell the actuality of their delay for he was to inform his seniors of Mary's invitation. He was relieved to find that their initial disgust with the two junior players quickly turned to back-slapping when they heard of the opportunity to display their thespian talents before a monarch, with fine food to follow.

The next two days were a whirl of activity taken up with rehearsals of their play and escorting their charges to the fair and around the other sights of York. Throughout this time Will's thoughts were never far from Bolton Castle, or more particularly its prisoner. He wondered what exactly Mary had thought of him, not much more than a boy really, *for she must be at least twenty years older than me* was his recurring thought. *She seemed to display affection towards me but this was more likely a consequence of her warm nature,* for Mary's charming character was legendary and she was admired not only by those of her own religious persuasion. *But those glances...and surely it was not merely protocol to request a farewell kiss of me. No...* Will decided *...there is definitely a glimmer of a chance that Marie is nurturing fond thoughts as am I.*

Such reveries had to be cast aside for Thursday afternoon arrived and all energies had to be directed towards the performance of the Mystery Play.

Their performance was well received by the motley audience but that evening's celebration of their success, in liquid form, resulted in sore heads for Will and Fulke on the Friday morning, for they had neither the capacity or experience of drinking ale that their older fellow-actors had.

Saturday morning was a time of even worse suffering for the duo but they had to lay to the task of loading the wagons and preparing for the return journey, which began shortly before noon.

That day they travelled as far as Masham but despite the arduous day Will slept but little that night for his mind was racing with thoughts of the morrow when he would once more meet his bewitching queen, for he now considered himself to be under a spell. *Can a man become so captivated after merely a few hours of a woman's company?* he pondered, for these emergent feelings were new to the young Shakespeare.

His musing was interrupted when a serious-faced Fulke appeared alongside and leapt up onto the seat of Will's wagon.

He looked at his colleague 'Why the frown Gyllom?'

After a pause of some seconds his friend replied, 'Shakespeare I know you to be a novice in the world of women...'

'And of course you have a vast experience'

'Well no, but I am I believe, aware of their feminine wiles, their manipulations'

'Where is this leading Gyllom?'

'Well...' and Fulke's face contorted as if in agony

'Come on man, is there something I should know?'

Fulke placed an arm round Will's shoulders and spoke in a low voice, 'Will fellow I know only that you are smitten by our newly-met monarch. I do not seek to enquire just how far you are fallen'

'And?'

'I share your appreciation, let's call it, of Queen Mary'

'So you see what I see in her?'

'Of course…but'

'But?' Shakespeare snapped

'I don't want to upset you Will boy'

'So?'

'Alright. Look you are just a…an ordinary-looking youngster, a teacher, no dazzling courtier'. Shakespeare was frowning now as Fulke proceeded. 'Look man what do you think there is about you to so rapidly attract a queen?'

'What are you saying Gyllom?'

Fulke pursed his lips then continued 'I can't help thinking about that lad in Scotland'. Now Will did look puzzled. 'That boy who helped Mary to escape, from Lochleven Castle I think it was'

'Yes, the Douglas boy nodded Will. 'Go on'

'Well is it not possible that she charmed him to use him?'

Will's interruption was curt 'Hey stop this Gyllom, I see what you're thinking. Well I don't feel used. You should see how she is with me when we are alone'

'William my fellow all women….alright let's drop it. Just don't get hurt my dear friend, or even worse as it could be in these treacherous times'

'I would risk my neck, my life, for Mary'

'I'll warrant she knows that'

'I hope she does. Now let it lie!'

Fulke shrugged his shoulders whilst assuring himself that he had at least tried to warn his friend.

Will broke a ten-minute silence during which Gyllom had remained beside him 'Anyway Marie has never mentioned escape'

'Alright, alright. I am probably wrong, but I truly care for you Shakespeare and I don't want to see your head leave your neck'.

The two young men meandered on, Will giving the occasional ill-tempered heavy flapping of the reins to the horse pulling them.

Fulke could not maintain the uneasy calm, he turned to Will, 'I will say this and I promise to talk no further on this matter. We Catholics, devotees of Queen Mary, all know her history, I am talking of her personal affairs. Will before she was thirty years of age...'

Will was almost shouting in anger 'Yes yes yes we know...three husbands, all dead, or Bothwell is as good as while he rots in that Danish jail'

'And Riccio?' Fulke offered. 'Stabbed to death in front of her with Darnley among the murderers. Will oh Will! Attachment to our Queen has been akin to a sentence of death, can you not see why I worry so?'

Shakespeare ended the discussion, 'We must pull over for the night Fulke. I thank you my dearest and most valued friend'.

Will spent a night without sleep, partly through his excitement at the prospect of meeting-up again with Marie but mostly having tortured thoughts as he mulled over the warning which Fulke had given him.

It had been decided that as it was Sunday the next day then a late arising was deserved, but as the sky lightened the fretful teacher was atop a nearby hill, straining his eyes pointlessly to the northwest. He wanted to rush down to their encampment and rouse everybody to make an early start but he knew this would be poorly received so he was forced to frustratedly kick his heels.

At this same hour Queen Mary was also awake, lying in her Flemish four-poster bed, abstractedly fingering the carvings as she contemplated the forthcoming day when she would meet with *mon bel garcon. It has been so long since I have felt a stirring in my heart. I pray that this time it will not mislead me for surely my choices since my poor tragic little Dauphin Francis were disastrous. Both Darnley and Bothwell desired me for my position, not for what I am. They wanted a queen in order to share a queen's power, not a woman with passions.* Her face lit up as she spoke aloud to herself 'I may be mistaken but I sense that young William is rather taken by me and solely by me as a person, for power is a thing long lost to me. Anyway, whatever, today should prove an enjoyable diversion, a welcome change from the drudgery of this place' and she threw back the covers and leaped joyously out of bed.

Will's heartbeat was increasing with every revolution of his wagon's wheels for they were on the last leg of the journey to Mary. The train of carts, now comprising four in number, was approaching the junction with the lane leading up to the village of Castle Bolton. As Will turned-in the leading cart he was startled as two women leaped out in front of him from behind a clump of trees around the corner, but then his surprise became delight as he recognised the object of his daydreams of the past six days. He jumped down from the wagon and knelt in front of Mary. She giggled delightedly before addressing him 'Will please don't be silly, get up lad'.

Looking rather sheepish, he got to his feet after kissing the proffered hand. Mary turned to glance at her young maidservant then asked Will 'Is Fulke not with you?'

He turned to call out 'Gyllom, come here man' and Fulke appeared from the final wagon and ran to join his friend.

Mary addressed him, with a mischievous smile on her lips 'Mr. Gyllom I present Mistress Bastion, one of Mrs. Bastions two daughters. You may call her Angelique. Its a French name, for her mother asked me to name her when she was born'.

Fulke was now the one in shock for Angelique was none other than the beautiful girl who had earned him a tapped ankle from Shakespeare when he had first seen her in the Solar. As he looked at her the young girl's mouth, which had already seemed oversized for her petite pale face, broadened further into a cute tight-lipped smile before she bashfully lowered her head to stare at her shoes. Fulke was left looking on a mass of blonde ringlets as her hair tumbled forward. He took the opportunity to absorb what a fine slender figure this lass had; she was almost a shorter replica of her beautiful mistress.

Mary spoke 'Angelique, if you can look up, I present Fulke Gyllom of Hoghton Tower. A notable scholar and actor' she added with another charming little giggle. Will's companion knelt in front of the girl and offered his hand, provoking a suppressed tittering from Angelique. Mary, after declaring a sincere 'charmant', turned back to Shakespeare 'Will cannot one of your fellows drive your cart up to the castle for I would walk with you'. It was several seconds before he reacted to this request, not having believed his own ears.

'Yes, yes. Richard would you take the reins' he called to the most responsible of his flock.

Mary spoke to her servant 'Angelique you must experience a ride on a horsecart, Fulke may she sit beside you?' The youth gleefully took the girl's hand and helped her up to the bench-seat. Shakespeare slapped the horse's neck and the procession moved off up the gentle slope to the castle, leaving a queen and her admirer alone in the lane.

Those amber eyes stared into Will's 'Did you enjoy your visit to York sir?'

Will appreciated this mock formality for it made their actual friendship all the sweeter. 'Your majesty...' *for two can play this game* he decided, '...I must confess that the audience was lacking one I wished were there'

'Ah so there is a Lancashire lass after all' teased Mary.

'Marie!' he pleaded, and the soulful expression on his face caused Mary to take pity on him, but smiling nevertheless as she did so. She quietly took his hand

'So you've missed your queen then Will?' He turned to look at her as they continued their slow stroll up the lane. He didn't speak but his look gave Mary the answer she had hoped for.

They reached the castle gates and Will prepared to take his hand from Mary's grasp but as she sensed this she gripped it even harder and submerged their coupling in the ample folds of her burgundy gown. Will saw that the courtyard had been transformed, for a huge marquee tent was occupying much of the compound. Mary smiled at him 'There you are Will, this shows I had confidence in your returning to perform for me, yes? This is the accommodation that I promised'

'Marie you could never have doubted that' and the monarch smiled inwardly at his comment.

Their reveries were interrupted as the ever-officious Brackenby strode towards them. 'Your majesty...'

'Mon Dieu Brackenby what is it now?'

'You were absent. I was not told. Then these travelling players arrived, together with your girl'

'Correct on all three counts Brackenby' she mocked sarcastically, 'Is there more?'

'Your majesty...', Will noted the increased reverence from the man on this occasion, concluding that a reprimand had been delivered from Scrope or Knowles. 'I could only reason that you had effected an escape when I saw you were not with your servant'

'Brackenby you are a fool, why would I abandon the hospitality I receive in Bolton Castle?' she answered, and Will had already learned enough of this woman to know that there would be a bulging of her tongue in her cheek. Brackenby skulked off, having lost yet another verbal exchange with this Scot with the razor-sharp mind and a quick wit. Mary squeezed Will's hand, which she had held secretly throughout, and shrugged her shoulders at him, a gesture which Will recognised as her physical expression of 'what a fool' or 'why does he bother?'.

Will's companions were milling around the courtyard, looking a little lost, but they turned as one when Will appeared, walking closely with the queen. A number of knowing nudges were silently made, as if to relieve their respective incredulities.

'Come lads, lunch is prepared for us' Mary called out to them, while Will once more revelled in the sound of her appealing accent which so enhanced the invitation.

A veritable feast of a cold buffet was ready in the Guest Hall and it was welcomed by the travellers who were flagging after their journey. Even Will's appetite had returned for he had forsaken breakfast due to his nervous excitement. The boys were permitted to sample the mulled wine, 'for medicinal purposes to extinguish the chills from the cold travel' explained Mary to a semi-protesting Will. Then she changed the subject 'The play will be performed in the Great Chamber Will, for that will allow for a measure of promenading. I extended invitations to the Lord and Lady Scrope and to Knowles, but he declined on the grounds that, and she adopted a mocking tone, 'the Mystery Cycle perpetuates the Catholic doctrine and I would consider myself less than loyal to my Queen should I attend'.' Another shrug. 'But that is of no consequence, the Scropes will attend. Come Will' and she led him through to the Solar, for they had ascended to the Guest Hall from another entrance. As they entered it Mary pointed to the far end of the room where Will could see two palliasses on the floor. 'You see sir that sleeping facilities have been provided for my two special guests'

'But...' began Will, whilst knowing that protest to this lady was pointless.

'Why Master Shakespeare I could not allow personal friends to sleep in a tent in the yard' she smiled. Will submitted, at the same time imagining the jealous teasing that he and Fulke could expect to receive from their colleagues. The couple walked back to the Guest Hall where the loud high-pitched voices were evidence of wine's effect on schoolboys. Luckily they were not required to take part in the forthcoming performance and most of them were sent to their marquee for an afternoon nap.

It was time for Will to join his fellow players in preparation, but his calm readiness was shattered as Mary kissed him fleetingly on the lips, whispering 'Play well for me Will' before leaving a dumbstruck actor and going to greet her noble 'guests', who were in fact her hosts.

The extract from the play lasted for almost two hours, and apparently held the attention of its audience, a throng which included Mary, Lord and Lady Scrope and the four Maries, the Marys Beaton, Fleming, Seton and Livingstone who had shared their lives with Mary since childhood when she had been sent to France as a five-year-old girl. Wherever Mary went they accompanied her, be it Scotland, France or England; a palace or a prison. Also amongst the spectators were most of the queen's retinue of fifty-one, with a privileged position, seated close to the four Maries, being accorded to Angelique Bastion with her mother and sister.

Enthusiastic applause greeted the closure of the afternoon's proceedings with congratulations being offered to all of the players. Mary came straight to her beau 'Oh Will you have a talent - but for playing a woman. I trust it was not too authentic' she taunted, 'for I would hope sometime to see you perform as a man'. Will coloured visibly at this last, partly because he was unsure if innuendo had been directed at him. 'Oh William I must not tease you so. We will await you in the Guest Hall. Come Maries' and as she swept out she turned to glance over her shoulder at a confused lad, whose face eventually broke into a smile to match hers.

The ensuing banquet was a grand affair with many items of food that the players had never seen before, all provided by Lord

Scrope. For Will however it was not an event to enjoy for some semblance of protocol had to be maintained and Mary's fondness of him, which he no longer doubted, could not be displayed publicly, so whilst she sat at the high table parlying politely with the Scropes and her Maries he found himself between Mary's Reader Mr. Prewe, a reserved man with no desire to converse, and the youthfully silent servant of Mr. Baron, her Physician. Flashing glances were snatched between he and Mary, usually causing Will to ask Mr. Prewe to repeat his occasional words. He envied his friend, for Fulke, not subjected to discretion, was seated between Mrs. Bastion's two daughters and was clearly enjoying himself, as were they, for they all three ate little but talked and laughed a lot.

Will was thankful when people started to leave the long table, many of his colleagues the worse for wear. The boys had been dispatched to bed after their own pre-banquet; perhaps as well for their 'superiors' did not now present a pleasant spectacle. *Even Fulke was a little too merry* thought Will, but then acknowledged that sour grapes had probably influenced this judgement. Lord and Lady Scrope, a couple who Will found to be most likeable and totally without airs, came to bid him goodnight and again praised the afternoon's performance. Eventually only Mary, Will and Fulke's group remained, then Gyllom left with his arm around Angelique's waist. Mary stood up and came to Will who was sitting disconsolately, and a little sulkily, looking into his wineglass. He looked up as she arrived beside him and spoke softly 'Will it was as painful for me. I too have waited six days for your company' and as she took his hand he pursed his lips and stood to face her. 'Come fellow let us talk awhile in my sitting-room' and she led him upstairs to what had been Lord Scrope's chamber before he had moved out into the Constable's Quarters. His wife, Mary had told Will earlier, had been a friend of hers but word was sent from London that, because of their closeness Lady Scrope should 'lay her belye elsewhere' and she subsequently moved out to a house some two miles from her own castle. As they entered Mary's inner sanctum Will was impressed by the huge Cloth of State which hung above her chair. 'Oh Will the trouble I had in getting them to send me that from Lochleven. I even had to plead for my clothes, for I left with only the taffeta dress I was wearing when dear George helped me to escape from that castle. He was only seventeen you know, and I think rather in love with me'. She smiled gently at the memory of the Douglas boy, perhaps seeing a parallel in tonight's companion. Will's unseen frown reflected his recalling of Fulke's advice, but he rapidly banished such thoughts as ridiculous negativity when Mary lightly laid her hand on his. As they sat talking Mary related some of the details of her eventful life. Will sat spellbound as this beautiful woman described a series of adventures that sounded almost incredible to his ears. 'Can you imagine Will being held prisoner by one's own Lords in the same castle where I had spent my honeymoon with that wretched Darnley. Do you know I even suffered a miscarriage, of twins, when I was first placed in the horrible Glassin Tower there, after which they moved me into the Tower House of the castle where at least I could sit in a window and sew, and look out at the loch. Will there is so much I could talk with you of, but what of you young man, for your history is ahead of you'. As they sat talking in the firelight Mary questioned him on his hopes for the future, both immediate and long-term. Will admitted to writing a little poetry and saw this perhaps as an alternative to his teaching duties, although he hoped to one day have his own company of actors, maybe even writing a play or two himself.

'And will you write of your meeting with a Scottish Queen Will?'

'Marie I hope it will be more than just a meeting for...' and he now felt the recklessness of desperation, aided confessedly by three goblets of claret, '...I have to see you again after tomorrow'.

Mary's face looked soft but sad 'My dear Will. That's sweet of you, but look at our ages. How old are you, sixteen, seventeen? whilst I am thirty-eight, thrice married, three times widowed before I was twenty-five'. She paused for his response.

'Marie I am not much more than a boy but meeting you has convinced me that numbers count for nothing in matters of the heart'

'Mon cher j'espere que c'est vrai' she murmured to him.

Mary Seton arrived to help her mistress prepare for bed and apologised for the interruption, having assumed that her queen was alone as usual. The queen signalled to her and as the loyal friend left Mary took Will's head and kissed him forcefully and uninhibitedly. 'Sweet dreams Will. We have tomorrow'. Will squeezed her hands this time before leaving in a daze, unconscious of Miss Seton's presence in the passageway as he passed her.

Fulke was already in his bed, beaming at Will as he arrived, 'Shakespeare I need a poem'.

Will did not smile, 'Mmm', then he undressed and climbed into his temporary bed.

'Will lad why so sad? Have you not enjoyed seeing your queen again?'

'Too much so Fulke. Goodnight'

'I would hazard that someone has been pierced by Cupid's dart' claimed his friend before turning away. 'Goodnight Shakespeare'.

'A minute Gyllom. Look you were wrong earlier. Marie has told me that she is dubious about my being too young, and she also talked of the Douglas boy. So you see she is not enticing me to help her escape'

'Alright fellow. I merely wished to warn you of what could befall. Goodnight again'

'Oh poppycock to you' scoffed Will testily, and he threw the covers over his head.

Hours later though he was still restlessly tossing, tortured by nagging doubts regarding Mary's reciprocation of his own amorous feelings. Was he, he asked himself, to be merely a fleeting diversion for his chestnut-haired goddess?

Chapter Six

They meandered slowly towards Leyburn, keeping to the tarmac for most of the way unless they saw a public footpath.

'What would you be doing tonight Sam if we hadn't met?'

Sam stopped and looked at Kate, 'I would have driven home to Barnard Castle, probably have poured myself a long scotch and perhaps crashed out in front of the telly'

'No girlfriend to report back to then?' she queried, with arched brow.

'No Kate, no girlfriend'

'Not interested?'

'What is this? Have you got Spanish blood in you?' he laughed

'Just female curiosity'

'Yes I'm sometimes interested, but its been two years since I was in a relationship, well a marriage actually. Sally, a nurse'. Kate waited for him to continue as they strolled slowly on. 'I was usually absorbed in my writing or research when she was around and then she worked funny hours anyway'

'Was that the problem then?'

'Perhaps the beginning of it, but then her hours got even funnier and I found out she was getting the bedside manner treatment from one of the doctors'

'Oh'

'Yes that's about what I said' he smiled. 'Somehow it wasn't too much of a surprise. We'd lost any common ground. Sally wasn't into history, or books at all really, and just how involved can you become in someone else's patients? Anyway since it appears to be inquisition time Mistress Kate are you half of an item as they say?'

'Well I go around with Dave, one of the lads I told you I go to Preston footy with, but there's not really a spark there, no raging passions. He's a physicist, all a bit calculating and unimaginative for me I'm afraid. But he's someone to share time with'. Kate took Sam's hand 'Come on let's get to Leyburn' and she accelerated their pace.

They both liked the look of an old coaching-inn in the town-centre and luckily there were vacancies.

'Two single rooms no sir. I have one left but my other spare is a family room, with a double and a single bed. Quite frankly, and I don't wish to be nosey, but I would suggest the family, it will cost less than two bookings'.

Sam looked tentatively at Kate. She grinned and turned to the middle-aged receptionist 'I suppose I could share a room with my father'. The woman's eyebrows rose a little at this but went even higher when the man slapped the girl's bottom. Kate was laughing, 'Sorry Sam but you looked so nervous'. Then she turned back to the waiting clerk, 'Yes we accept your suggestion, the family room, and he's not really my dad - we met on your doorstep'. This time the woman knew not to believe Kate and all three of them laughed together, two of them knowing that the duration of their acquaintance was in fact only a little longer.

The room was huge with a large bay-window overlooking the square. Sam was studying the beds and he walked across to the single in the far corner, 'I'll take this one' he offered.

'No why should you have to Sam. This is supposed to be a time of equal rights so I'll spin you for it' and Kate took a tenpenny piece from her jeans.

'Tails' called Sam

Kate looked down at the carpet, 'Looks like you're the one with the space sir' and she threw her backpack onto the small bed. Sam started to politely protest but Kate halted him. 'If there's going to be an argument Mr. Woodhouse we'll have to share the big one, so look out' she added with a twinkle in her eye. 'Sam as you've won can I have first shower?'

'Course' he smiled, 'What is it they say? Age before beauty' and he ducked to avoid the cushion she threw at him. Then she stood looking at him with her hands on her hips

'Are you going to wait there for me to come out of the shower?'

Sam was flustered, 'Oh of course, I'll wait for you in the bar shall I?' and he walked to the door, leaving a perhaps despondent-looking Kate in the middle of the room.

Chapter Seven

Will woke up, suddenly, not knowing why. It was still night and the embers of the fire which had been lit for their benefit still cast a light over the room, He turned to his left and saw that Fulke's bed was empty and he had a good idea why that was so, 'flown away with his little angel' he concluded.

He had lain awake for some ten or fifteen minutes when he tensed up, for there, on the opposite wall, was a huge shadow moving across the room. It stopped and Will could discern that it was of human form. The person, whoever it was, reached to it's head and pulled off a nightcap, releasing a cascade of hair. The shadow continued across the wall in Will's direction and then he heard that whispered accent 'Will, are you awake?'

'Marie?'

'Oui mon cher, c'est moi'

Will's heart was pounding as he sat up and looked to his right. He saw a vision that would forever hold a place in his memory. Standing there with her red hair haloed by the firelight, and with the outline of her body clearly visible through the transparentised nightgown, was Mary Queen of Scots. Will felt himself stirring as she came to his side and reached down for his hand 'I cannot sleep

Will, knowing that you are down here. Would you come to my chamber?'

He clambered to his feet and took her in his arms, knowing that she would feel his reaction, and this knowledge brought that sexy smirk back to her face, 'Oh William you are pleased to see me yes?'.

'I'm sorry Marie'

'Never ever be sorry for your emotions Will. They are what show you are alive, and you seem to be very lively sir. Come with me *mon amour*'. Then as she turned she paused teasingly to allow her young man to appreciate the outline of her still-firm breasts. Will noted also how tall and slim she truly was when not clad in bulbous gowns. *She must be six feet* he decided, trying to have rational thoughts. Mary reached back for his hand and led him out of the Solar, past the nursery where her Maries were sleeping, and up the steps to her bedroom. She turned round and kissed him. 'This bed is still a virgin Will. I think it has been so for long enough'.

Will felt himself to be a willing pawn as Mary walked across her chamber, turned to face him and slid her nightdress off her shoulders to fall to the floor. Then her long legs brought her slowly to the frozen yet boiling Will and she pulled his gown over his head before wrapping him in her arms. 'Oh Will how I want you, *je toi desire*. Come to my bed *mon cher* '.

The bed was not the only virgin in the room and Will was overwhelmed by the touch of a woman's skin as Mary took his hand and guided it onto her waist, then upwards to release it as she reached her left breast. Will had had his adolescent fantasies as to what such a moment might be but nothing had prepared him for the sensations he now felt. Mary sensed his tentativeness, 'Darling Will am I your first?'. Will slowly nodded as they gazed into each other's eyes. 'Then my sweetheart let the teacher be taught'.

Their hours of slow and gentle lovemaking were a progression to a frantic finale that both had needed for different reasons; Mary glorying in an act that she had thought never to enjoy again, with all the fury of suppressed passions released, and Will gaining the confidence to fully satisfy his tutor as this incredible woman showed him how to lose himself and revel in the female body, his teenage imaginings of the past being far surpassed by the reality.

Afterwards they lay quietly stroking each other, Mary emitting occasional groans which puzzled Will as his hands roamed over her body. Finally, with his head cradled in the nest between Mary's neck and shoulder, he drifted off to sleep, with Mary, now more relaxed than any time she could remember, swiftly following him

Chapter Eight

Sam was enjoying an Irish malt when Kate entered the bar. She looked gorgeous in a deep green satin dress that clung to her, all the way down to nine inches above her knees. 'It's weird you know, my friends asked me why the hell I should pack my oomph dress to go on a hiking holiday. I must have been psychic eh Sam?'

'In what way?' he ventured

'You know, that I would end up in a posh hotel' she answered with a trace of a tongue-in-cheek smirk. Anyway sir are you ready for your shower?'

'Oh yes, but what can I get you to drink first?'

'I'll think about it. You go upstairs'

Sam indulged himself in a long shower, spending the time thinking over the day's developments. *Christ she looked incredible in that frock, some girl I reckon. Behave Samuel you almost could be her father* he reminded himself and determined that she was just enjoying a day's flirting.

Through habit he wrapped his towel around his waist as he stepped out of the bathroom, an act he had cause to be thankful of, for the room was not empty when he entered it. Sitting expectantly in one of the sumptuous armchairs was a very sexy-looking female holding a wineglass. She wore a green dress.

'Kate!'

'Sam! Well you were a long time so I thought I'd better check you hadn't fallen in the shower or something. Nice suntan' and she leant back and stretched her arms out, at the same time giving Sam a maximum view of her thighs. Then Sam was relieved to hear her ask 'Are you hungry? I'm famished. Must be the air. Shall we go and eat?'

The air crackled with released tension together with a certain amount of regret at avoiding what they both knew could have happened.

As they sat waiting in the dining-room Sam was not at all hungry. The only way to recover his appetite would be to divert his thoughts to the top half of his body. He tried to ignore the pair of bare legs that had accidentally found their way between his own. Actually a serious question had occurred to him during the afternoon. He put on the most earnest face he could muster, 'Kate'

'Sam?'

'No listen this might interest you'

'I'm all ears'

'Stop that and listen' he laughed as the errant legs massaged his. Kate opened her large eyes even wider in mock expectation of his pearls of wisdom. He began, 'What if your theory about Shakespeare is correct and he was living up here when Mary Queen of Scots was imprisoned in the north?'

Kate looked a little disappointed at this diversion but she knew Sam was seriously interested in her own studies and that had to be extremely positive. But that didn't stop her thinking '*This guy*

I could really go for'. Then she opened her mouth 'What are you saying Sam?'

'Well if he was a catholic'

'Yes'

'And he toured with the players of Lord Hoghton or whatever his name was'

'Mmm'

'Why shouldn't he have met one of the most famous Roman Catholics in history?'

Now Kate really was listening. 'You mean...'

'Yes, its not inconceivable that he visited Bolton Castle while she was imprisoned there. I mean its not a million miles from Hoghton is it? I want to go back there, there's something I saw today which I want to check out'

'Shit Sam what was it?'

'Kate I'll tell you tomorrow if you come back there with me. Till then its a secret'

'You're rotten Sam Woodhouse. But you're special with it'

Sam warmed at this comment and he decided to order some food before his digestive juices stopped flowing again. 'Shall we order madam?'

'Umm, I see we could have oysters for starters' but she was laughing as she said this, knowing that Sam had no need of aphrodisiacal supplements from the way he had looked at her in this dress. He had thought she hadn't noticed his reaction in the bedroom. 'Honestly Sam I'm not that hungry now, I think I'll just have the plaice'

'I'll follow you Kate'

'What all the way?' she teased and the leg-rubbing resumed.

Less than a minute later she leant across the table with her mouth pouting, 'Oh shit Sam I'm ravenous, lets go upstairs' and the newly-arrived waiter was experienced enough to pretend he had heard nothing and wheeled round again without stopping at their table, although wearing a smile on his return trip.

They did not exactly run up the plush-piled staircase but almost. Kate still had the key and she flung the door open and shut it after Sam with a long leg. She spun round to face him 'Sam I want you, take me to bed will you?' and she turned her back for him to unzip the skin-tight dress. Sam slid it off her shoulders to reveal a bra-less back, then Kate waggled her hips as she slid the satin down and off to show that she was a girl with minimalist beliefs. Sam's fleeting thought was *Do they still call that a g-string?* before Kate turned to unbuckle his belt. Her breasts were small and firm, Sam was delighted to see as he felt his trousers being removed. Kate slowly unbuttoned his shirt, all the while rubbing the length of her body against him. Finished her face was beaming, 'Your bed or mine?' she whispered, taking his hand and leading him to the king-size.

Sam was recovering his calm after the frantic dash from the dining-room. Time for him to play a role, 'Hey slowly, *piano, piano!*' he suggested with what he considered to be panache.

His words went unheeded though as Kate tugged off his pants before literally ripping off her own flimsy garment. 'Sam time for calm afterwards. I have to fuck you now, quickly, come on!' She grabbed his hand, at the same time tugging the duvet off the bed and throwing it across the room before flinging her own slender body on the sheet. 'Do you want me Sam?'

The answer had been swift and vigorous. They lay panting. Kate reached across and stroked his sweating brow. 'O.K. Sam what did you say piano, piano?'. What are you some sort of musical pervert?' she laughed. 'Anyway we couldn't really have done that in the hotel lounge you know'

Sam tittered like a schoolboy, not far from how he felt at this moment. 'Oh Kate, Kate, Kate, I've found a perfect mate' he muttered then heaved a sigh.

'Such poetry Mister Shakespeare' she chuckled.

He turned her over on the crumpled sheet and softly patted her bottom - this was the prelude to a long and sleepless night.

Chapter Nine

Mary Seton was humming to herself as she wandered into her mistress' bedchamber but she jolted to a stop when she looked towards the bed. Her shock was a happy one though as she gazed at this sleeping couple, the young lad and the queen each with an arm around the other. She turned on her heel and rushed back down to the nursery-room, to the other Marys, wanting to share her exciting discovery. Moments later four heads were peering round the angle of the doorway.

Will woke, at first believing he was still in a pleasurable dream, the one he had had for the past week, for he was lying in a four-poster bed beside the woman of his desires. He gently brushed a red wisp of hair from where it had fallen across Mary's eyes and was gazing enrapturedly into her face when she too stirred, blinked, and smiled up at him, 'Bonjour mon amour '. Will didn't speak he just leaned down and kissed her eyes. 'Will my darling I see you are learning the ways of a lover'

'How could I fail with such an excellent and royal tutor?' he smiled.

Mary pulled his head down onto her breasts, running her fingers through his hair, 'I will never forget this night William, that I can promise you. We will always have that memory whatever else becomes of both of us'. He craned his neck up to see those amber eyes looking into the distance of nowhere. She turned to gaze impassively at him, 'And what of today mon cher? Are you to leave me?'

Will's face looked tragically up at her 'How can I Marie? I have to be with you' he pleaded.

'Darling Will I fear that cannot be so, you have your master to return to. You must not spend your time in a prison'

He laughed lightly 'Such a sentence would be welcomed by any man I feel'

A crowing cockerel was a herald to further amours as the couple once again enjoyed each other.

It was almost nine o'clock when a nervous Mary Seton was heard calling a discreet 'Your majesty' from the passageway.

'Un moment Marie. Je vous appellerai quand je veux me preparer'

Will turned to her 'I must find my fellows, although I suspect that sore heads will be keeping them abed awhile' he grinned. 'Fulke I know not of for he was absent last night before you came to me'

Mary was smiling 'I think perhaps a winged cherub might have born him to heaven' but she did not disclose on whose advice Angelique had acted. Will climbed out of the sumptuous bed and as he did so Mary's question was surprising, 'William do you carry a knife?'

He looked at her and grinned as he stood there naked 'Not about me at this moment ma'am'.

Mary's raucous laugh was heard in the nursery downstairs. 'Why sir you mock me, what liberties you do take - especially of a night' she added with sparkling eyes.

Will was enjoying her pleasure in him but he had to ask 'For what purpose a knife, how do you say - ma cherie?'

'Bravo Will, parfait! No I wish to commemorate our night when we deflowered my bed'

Will was still puzzled but promised to obtain a knife during the morning. He had slid his nightgown on over his head when Mary got out of the bed and lifted his garment, pressing their bodies together before putting on her own nightdress. She took his hand and led him across her chamber to the arch of the doorway. They kissed long and hard. 'A bientot my Will'. He stroked her cheek before stealthily descending the stairway, cautiously pausing before dashing past the entrance to the nursery which adjoined the Solar where the Maries were.

Fulke was lying in bed and sat up as Will approached. 'Aha Master Shakespeare. I was not aware that you suffered from the habit of sleep-walking' he beamed, 'or did you prefer to sleep in the tent with your fellows?'

Will did not take the bait, realising that Fulke must have guessed as to his actual whereabouts. Instead he launched a counter-offensive 'Why no Master Gyllom, I awoke in the night and seeing your empty bed I feared for your safety and went looking. Thankfully you are now found'

Fulke was laughing furiously 'Shakespeare you are as mad as me, and as good a liar. But tell me sir, methought you a virgin boy'

'So I was sir, and let that be an end of the matter'

'An end to coincide with yours eh Will?' chuckled his friend. 'But to lose it with a queen - that's something my man. Anyone else will be slumming now would they not?'

'There will never be an 'anyone else' my friend' Will assured him

'Ah Will would it that life were that simple' Fulke sighed with all the apparent wisdom of an elderly sage.

Shakespeare was smiling as he counter-teased 'Anyway my wandering friend how was life among the celestial ones?'. Fulke looked mystified. 'Celestial - angels - Angelique!' Will explained.

Gyllom grinned but said nothing, then leaping to his feet he said 'Come get dressed man and we will search for our companions and seek breakfast, or has a royal petit dejeuner already been taken?'. Will leaped on his mate and they fell wrestling and laughing to the floor.

Their actor-companions were a sorry sight. The huge tent appeared to be a hospital with a series of men wandering around holding their heads or dashing outside to vomit. The boys were all highly amused by the scene. Will was not sympathetic, he yelled out in a loud voice 'Come fine fellows cooked breakfast awaits you, pork and eggs for everyone of you?'. The tirade of curses provoked mirth amongst Will and Fulke, then they fled outside as a fusillade of pillows was hurled in their direction.

They skidded to a halt as they met another occupant of the courtyard. 'Why Will, Fulke, good morning to you gentlemen. I trust you spent a comfortable night each of you?'. Will could not answer, he was not yet that good an actor, Mary obviously surpassing him also in that activity.

Fulke was the one to reply 'Yes thank you your majesty. Shakespeare was earlier agreeing with me that it was the best night of his life'. Will was glowering at his treacherous friend.

'Why sirs I'm well glad to hear such news. So you slept well aye Will?'.

He looked at her, a picture of sublime innocence. His smile could be held back no longer, 'Yes thank you your majesty. I would that all other nights would be as so'

'And did you dream sir?'. Will felt sure that she knew that Fulke would be aware. She was revelling in this facade, this game.

'I know not if I dreamed Marie, for certain events seemed more than real, a fantasy realised even'

'I'm pleased to hear that William. Shall we meet at breakfast?' Then she shattered the pretence as she teasingly asked 'And you won't forget the knife sir?' and smirked brazenly before walking away, leaving Gyllom open-mouthed as he turned queryingly to his friend.

Breakfast in the Solar was a poorly attended affair, there being only Mary, the two friends and the eight schoolboys. Not one of the other players managed an appearance. Mary sat with Will at the far end of the table, this prompting comments and nudges amongst the youngsters. Richard Appleby was bold enough to ask Fulke 'Sir is Mister Shakespeare befriended of the Scottish Queen?'

Fulke looked serious 'I think befriended is a safe word Dick, yes'.

Sam Baker was less cautious 'Fulke I think they are in love don't you?'.

Fulke stared at him, trying to hold a straight face, 'Samuel what was it that Queen Mary told you the other day?, 'telling tales is dangerous' wasn't it?'. Sam now knew that he had been correct in his assessment.

A hush fell over the room as a late entrant arrived, it was Seth Beardsley, the leader of the players. He presented a sorry figure as he walked in slowly and stooping. He saw Will sitting with the queen so he approached Fulke. He spoke softly and measuredly

'It's no good Gyllom, we none of us can travel today, we all perhaps indulged ourselves last night'. Fulke tried not to smile at this pitiful messenger.

He asked 'But Seth will we not already be considered overdue at Hoghton?'.

Beardsley lifted his drooping head again, 'That matter is taken care of Fulke. James Goodyear was suffering the least so I have sent him on one of our pack-horses to Hoghton Tower. He is to tell them that we have been delayed due to a wagon tumbling from the track, and that we might yet be a day or so in rebuilding it. They are to expect us when they see us'.

Fulke was delighted at this, albeit for personal reasons, for such a decision meant one more day in the company of sweet Angelique. 'Fine Seth, you return to your bed for now but we may have to move the wagons outside the castle walls for we cannot presume upon our host. I will inform Shakespeare of this matter'. The sad figure retreated to a chorus of titters from the pupils.

The boys finished their breakfast. Richard Appleby approached Fulke 'Sir if we are not leaving today may we play football on the green?'

'Yes Dick but watch out for the village boys. I want no broken limbs to tend to'.

Fulke approached the couple at the end of the room who were engrossed in conversation, but Will had seen Beardsley talking with Fulke. 'What did Seth want? He looks ill'

'As are all the others Will. He has sent word to Hoghton that we will not arrive today for they are too sick to travel. I told him we will move our carts into the village'.

Mary turned to him 'To the village Fulke, why so?'

'Your majesty we have enjoyed your hospitality but we must not presume on you further'

Mary pretended to look indignant 'Gyllom don't be foolish. You will remain here - by royal command if need be' she laughed. Fulke walked away a lot happier than he had approached.

'But Marie...' began Will before she put her fingers across his lips

'Alright Master Shakespeare tell me you would rather be away from me, yet in sight, than by my side'. Will's heart lifted even higher. Her voice changed tone 'Do you ride Will?'

'I can stay on a horse's back Marie - but not at your speed' he quickly added.

'Then this morning we shall go to the hills and enjoy the sunshine'. Will readily accepted another royal command

An hour later he was walking round the courtyard with a strange gait, stretching his legs sideways and crouching down, all in an effort to accustomise himself to the riding breeches which had been given to him by Mr. Curle. Mary appeared, also dressed in the attire of a man but no doubts as to her gender were left by the way she filled the red and green bodice and matching leggings. Will looked at her, stupefied as ever by this woman, 'Marie you are surely the most comely man on this earth'. She smiled and performed a coquettish turn to show him the back of her outfit.

'Will did you not know that one of my customs is to dress as a man. I am quite famed for it, so much more comfortable than those cumbersome gowns'

'But when we first met?'

'A secret Will' she whispered, although there was no-one else around, 'I was wearing the green riding-habit yes?'. Will nodded, recalling the impact of her first appearance. 'Well under that dress

I wore these breeches, for I always ride in the male style, astride my mount. Today with you I wear only the trousers'. Three horses were led into the yard. Will looked enquiringly at Mary. 'Of course they cannot possibly let me ride without a guard can they?' She frowned as she said this sarcastically and shook her head, 'But I will instruct him to keep his distance from us'. Will loved the idea of the prisoner giving instructions to the jailer. Mary's magnificent black stallion was dancing; rattling the cobbles and proving a handful for the groom. Will's animal, a bay of barely sixteen hands, appeared to be more sedate.

They were joined by Brackenby who climbed up onto his grey. 'Where to your majesty?'

'Why Brackenby to Scotland of course' she laughed. Brackenby coloured - again the butt of Mary's mocking wit.

They walked their horses out of the gates and jogged down to the Leyburn road then straight across it and up a steep incline. Mary led the way for the route was of course to be her choice. They reached a spot close to where they had first met, Mary pulled up and turned 'How goes it Will?'

'A little bumpy. I feel my rear will suffer tonight'

'Then you will need a comfortable bed to recover in' she smirked before urging her horse into a canter and riding off, leaving Will still stationary. She called back to him 'Come on my man, follow your woman'.

Brackenby, who had obeyed orders to never be closer than fifty yards, had heard none of this conversation from his position, but he had begun to wonder exactly what the relationship was between the Scottish Queen and this travelling player.

The exhilaration of riding was new to Will once he had mastered how to cope with it, for his only previous equestrian experiences had been astride cart-horses around Stratford. Mary halted again on the ridge, 'Will if you don't mind waiting awhile I want to give Jupiter a strong gallop. Can you wait for me?'

'Forever!' he smiled, which earned him a semi-embarrassed slap on his thigh from Mary before she headed off into the distance. Moments later Brackenby sped past the motionless Will, anxious that this whole expedition should not prove to be a preconceived escape attempt.

Twenty minutes later Mary returned, panting in synchrony with her horse. She looked radiant with glowing cheeks and hair dishevelled, for she had not dressed it up this morning and wore no cap. Will fell even deeper as he absorbed the sight of her.

'Are you alright William?' she called, seeing his serious countenance

'Fine Marie, except I am in love'.

Mary rode up close to him actually cast her eyes downwards, then, looking softly into Will's, she replied in her gentle voice 'Why thank you kindly sir'. Then she walked on with Will's horse matching strides alongside.

After several minutes of riding in silence Mary turned to him, 'You are not alone Will' and she reached across and grasped his hand.

Chapter Ten

A cockerel announcing another day was the last sound that Sam and Kate heard before they drifted off to sleep.

The next sound was the singing of a bright pink-haired chamber-maid as she walked into their bedroom. In a soft Scottish accent she quickly apologised '...cuz its half-past ten and usually there's nebuddy aboot at this time. I'll coom back'. She looked down at this silent naked couple who were still lying face down, the man with an arm across the girl's back. The young woman slowly reached behind her with one hand and reached for a covering duvet but it was lying on the far side of the room. They heard the door click shut behind their mid-morning alarm caller, then they briefly looked at each other before jointly bursting out laughing and flinging their arms around each other. The door burst open again and the maid, flashing her big bright eyes announced 'Oh by the way, in case you were wondering – your room today was prepared by Jessie!' Then she gave the pair a dazzling smile and went out the door.

'I suppose we've missed breakfast'

Kate gazed at him 'Well we can always have it in bed' and she threw herself on top of Sam.

They discovered that they could in fact take brunch if they wished but Kate and Sam both elected for cappucini and brioches in the lounge, Kate remarking as they entered 'Ooh look Sam there is a piano'. They chose the table in the bay-window. Kate looked at him with a straight face as she asked him 'Right my horny detective what were you saying about Bolton Castle before you dragged me upstairs for sex last night?'.

Sam choked on his brioche, partly at the impudence of Kate's role-reversal of what had actually happened but moreso because he shared hearing her words with an elderly pair of dowagers at the next table who were now staring at them with mouths agape. Sam smiled an obviously exaggerated apologetic grin at them then muttered to Kate 'Look you were the siren madam' at the same time squeezing hard on her left thigh under the table, provoking a delighted squeal. More head-turns before the ladies each cleared a throat, folded a napkin and stood up to leave a room which had suddenly become an annexe of Sodom and Gomorrah.

'No Sam, come on let's get serious' but Kate was still smiling.

'I want to go back to that carved bed we saw.

Kate adopted an accent from the Deep South 'Samuel Woodhouse why you're truly insatiable I do declare'.

'Behave woman! Do you want me to tell you or not?' he chuckled.

'I'm sorry Sam, I'm just so happy. Tell me on the way. Shall we pay the bill before we get thrown out of here?' Sam looked at this fantastic girl. She continued 'And I'm splitting it ok.? We shared a bed so we'll share its cost'. Sam was relieved to discover that this time they had no audience.

They went into town shopping for a picnic to eat on their journey, for they had decided to walk it again, leaving Sam's car where it was, then he would run her over to Hawes in the evening. Sam relished wandering round the shops holding hands with this beautiful young woman who he noticed had caused several appreciative heads to swivel.

The hotel had kindly let them leave their backpacks there for the day and they set off back towards Castle Bolton shortly after one o'clock. The sun was at it's hottest and both of them had put on tee-shirts and shorts, looking an established couple.

After a brisk walk out of the town Kate spoke 'Right Mr. Sam - the bed, what about it?'

'Yes. Kate you know how we climbed over the barrier rope to get a closer look at it'

'Mmm'

'Well how close did you look? - at the carving for example'

'Well it was clever, but nothing special was it? The guide-book said it was Flemish'

'I know that's what fooled me for a time. I think its older than I thought. I reckon Queen Mary Stuart actually slept in it'

'What!'

'Wait till we get there'.

Kate's curiosity had been roused, now Sam had left her in suspense. 'You devil, tell me'

'No, let it be a surprise. I may be wrong anyway'.

Kate tried to tickle the waist she was holding but Sam ran off and flung himself on the grass verge. As she caught up with him she asked 'Ready for a picnic in this field?'

'I'm not really hungry yet'

'Nor am I Sam - ready for a picnic in this field?'.

The bag of food, still untouched, was left with the lady in the ticket-booth of the castle. She remembered them from yesterday. 'Today the castle is just as deserted' she told them. When Sam asked for permission to have a close look at the Flemish Bed she telephoned through to Sir Harry and he readily gave his approval as soon as he realised that she was talking about the 'window-opener' who he had met yesterday. He also instructed her to grant them free admission.

Kate and Sam made straight for Mary's bedchamber and moved aside the red rope. Sam led her across the room. She looked at him expectantly.

'Kate you see how all the panels of this bed are carved beautifully, obviously by an expert craftsman; these three figures on the footboard for example'. Kate nodded. 'Well look here, and he took her hand and walked round to the high headboard which extended right up to the canopy. A draping of mediaeval cloth covered the flanks of it but Sam pointed to some lettering in the central panel. 'What do you see Kate?'

'A 'W', an 'M' and a sort of snake or something in the middle'

'Yes. I thought yesterday - Ah Flemish therefore William of Orange and Mary, you know the rulers of England after James the Second and before Queen Anne'

'Logical' she remarked

'But Kate look really closely at the carving of those letters. No Flemish expert did those'

'Graffitti Sam?'

He smiled, 'Yes graffitti, or sort of I think. But what's really got to me, thinking about it on our way to Leyburn yesterday is...'. He paused melodramatically for effect.

'Sam tell me for Christ's sake' she pleaded.

'Right, well I reckon that figure in the middle isn't a serpent or an 'and'. I bet its an 'F' as an old-style 'S'.' Kate could see where he was going, Sam spoke her thoughts 'What was the surname of the Bard?'

Kate began to smile 'Shakespeare - with an S. And Mary's was Stuart - with an S ', she had got in first. They exchanged a high-five then, for no apparent reason than joint exhilaration they hugged each other. Kate said it again 'William Shakespeare and Mary Stuart'

'In this bed?' posed Sam.

'Oh shit Sam what if you're right?'

'Kate there's a whole Ph.D. in this for you'

'You're not kidding!' and she took his head in her hands and kissed him hard and long. As they separated again she gave out a dirty laugh.

'What's up?' smiled Sam

'Well its sort of spooky don't you think, but doesn't it make you want to try the bed out?'

On cue as yesterday they were joined by the Honourable Harry, 'I think that would be extending my generosity too far don't you' he grinned. Sam had thought Kate incapable of looking embarrassed but at this moment she was scarlet.

'What have you discovered? Anything interesting?' the owner asked

'Well it depends' answered Sam' I've got a little theory but it would be stupid of me to tell anyone until I can check it out'

'Ok' said Harry unconcernedly. 'Have you finished in here?'

'Oh yes, sorry! But thanks a million for letting us look at the bed. I promise to let you know if anything comes of my idea'.

The trio shook hands and the Honourable Harry went up the steps towards the roof. As he reached halfway-up he stopped and looked back over his shoulder at them 'Yesterday afternoon you told me you are just good friends, do you think that 'just good friends' should really be trying out beds together?'. Sam and Kate looked at each other and burst out laughing. Harry shook his head and continued his ascent.

'What now Sam?'

He looked at her, feeling a little perplexed, 'Back to Leyburn I guess'

'We can have our picnic on the way'

'Kate you'll wear me out, I'm not used to this pace'

'Nor me Sam, honestly, but I really did mean eating' she replied, putting on a strange expression, a sort of superior innocence. Then she flung her arms round his neck for a quick tongue-probing kiss before taking his hand. He pulled her to a halt and she turned,

'Kate take a good look at that bed because if our theory proves correct then I promise you that one way or another the next time we see it we'll make love in it'.

Kate was not smiling as she spoke softly 'A girl could fall in love with you Sam. Come on fella' and she dragged him away.

Chapter Eleven

Mary and Will had almost reached the bottom of the lane up to the castle when they saw two figures lying in the grass enjoying the sunshine. As they drew close Fulke cried out 'Shakespeare I've lost my wager with young Angelique, I warranted that the two of you had eloped and were at this moment heading towards Durham'.

Mary looked down at him with a puzzled expression, 'Mister Gyllom why should that be so? Mister Shakespeare is merely my good friend'. She still wore a straight face, convincing Will once again what a natural actress she was. 'I trust sir that you have not spread gossip otherwise?'

Fulke now looked the recalcitrant schoolboy as he dropped his head, then looked up and answered 'Certainly I have not your majesty, I was just jesting with Angelique here'.

Mary maintained her serious countenance even while pronouncing 'Fulke you would do well to remember that my relationship with Will is as innocent as is yours with fair Angelique'. Now she laughed and Gyllom broke into a relaxed smile. The girl just sat and turned deep pink.

In the afternoon Mary showed Will the way up onto the castle roof. Their idyll in the sunshine was interrupted by the calling of

Mary's name by Mary Livingstone. Her plaintive voice grew louder as she climbed up to join them. She breathlessly announced 'Oh Marie here you are. We have been searching everywhere for you for Knowles is in a temper. He wishes to speak with you 'of a most important affair' he said, but cannot find you'.

Mary looked worriedly at Will then turned to her friend 'Thank you Marie. You may tell Knowles that I will meet him in the Solar at four o'clock. Oh and Marie...' she added, '...do not tell him where you found me'. The loyal companion's head disappeared through the roof-opening. 'Will what can be so urgent? I am a little disturbed. 'Why can they not leave us in peace?'. Then she looked intently into his eyes 'And why couldn't I have met you fifteen years ago?'

Will tried to lift her spirits 'Perhaps Marie because I was still in my mother's arms'.

She slapped him then hugged him, 'Mon cher cheri Will. Perhaps we had better go down to our fate'. They kissed passionately then Mary pulled away and with a smile announced 'By the way I have ordered your palliass to be removed from the Solar. Where will you sleep tonight Mister Shakespeare?'

Will was beaming as he took her hand and walked towards the hatch.

Sir Francis Knowles was pacing up and down the Solar and spun on his heel as Mary and Will entered. He put on his most official and pompous voice 'Mary Queen of the Scots I am to inform you that I have received word that you are shortly to be removed from Bolton Castle and will be taken to Tutbury Castle in Staffordshire'

Mary gasped and looked horrifiedly at Will. 'Mais non! Non! Pourquoi?' she asked Knowles

'Because your majesty it is felt that you have an excess of freedom of movement here and Tutbury will be more secure'. He spoke this last word with relish. Mary flung her head against Will's chest, not caring what Knowles should think of it. She was almost weeping as she turned to ask over her shoulder 'But when? When Knowles?'

'As soon as is practicable, probably in two weeks from now'. Then the ignorant man, without a word of farewell, strode out of the room.

'Oh Will will they never leave me at peace? I got used to confinement at Carlisle after the initial shock, then here at Bolton I have just acclimatised myself to a new way of life and now they are tearing up my feeble roots again' and she sobbed as she clung to him. Will was stuck for words, he too was devastated by this news. Mary spoke again 'I have heard tell of Tutbury. It is said to be a bleak and bitterly cold spot. Oh darling Will what will we do? You know I have fallen in love, a thing I never expected again in this life. At least at Hoghton you are not beyond a day's ride or two from me if you wished to visit me, but Tutbury!' Then, calling on her famed resilience and grit, she brought a weak smile to her face and with her lips inches from his whispered 'But mon cher we must enjoy what time we have today...' and she paused before making it a full smile and grabbing his hands she burst into a whirling dance and literally shouted out for all the world '...and tonight!', causing Will to marvel yet again at this chameleonesque female.

After the evening meal Mary and Will bid goodnight to Fulke who was surprised at their departure at the relatively early hour of seven o'clock, but Mary explained to him that 'We have affairs to discuss' adding quickly 'and not only affairs of the heart Mister

Gyllom. I trust you will spend a pleasant evening. You will have the privacy of the Solar to yourself tonight. Unless you wish to share it with anyone' she coyly added as she left the room. She did not see the suggestive gesture made by Fulke to Will as he followed his queen.

They went to her sitting-room and shared a sofa. 'Dear Will I have a proposal'. He looked expectantly at her. 'I just cannot be subjected to Tutbury's conditions'

'No?'

'No. I intend, with your help if you are prepared to assist me, to escape from Bolton before they move me'.

Will was stunned; once again this woman had struck him dumb with surprise, but this time it was tinged with apprehension as he once again recalled Fulke's warning. But he showed no sign of this concern as he asked eagerly 'Marie how can that be?'

'Will I know that your employer Sir Alexander Hoghton is sympathetic to my cause', Will nodded, 'Then would he not shelter me if I were to return to his home tomorrow with you?'.

Will did not answer straight away, his mind was racing. Eventually he spoke 'Marie I think you will agree that our fondness for each other is now broadly known here at Bolton'. Mary nodded a tacit agreement. 'Therefore should you disappear tomorrow, the very day that I and my fellows leave, then only one conclusion will be drawn, that you are with me. Travelling slowly in our wagons you would be hunted down within the hour'. Mary looked disappointed but her spirits rose when Will confirmed 'However my love have no doubts that I will help you away from here, but we must be more devious'. He acknowledged to himself that he was to some extent playing for time.

Mary looked worried again 'But how Will? What will we do?'

Will was surprised at his own resourcefulness and concluded that it must have been fired by his passion for this amazing woman, 'I have it Marie. As we know they will in all likelihood assume when you are not here that you are travelling to join me'

Mary was waiting with her beautiful eyes wide open 'Yes Will and...?'

'And..., I have it! We must lay a decoy, yes. We will give some deliberate intimation, some clue, that you are heading in the opposite direction'

'Oh my darling what genius for such a young and tender brain'.

Will looked embarrassed by her exaggeration, whilst perhaps surprising himself by his own cunning. Then he brought a note of circumspection to their proposals as he reminded Mary that 'Of course Marie none of this can be undertaken unless Sir Alexander approves of it'

'No' she said slowly, slowly enough for Will to rethink.

He now spoke in an equally pedestrian manner, 'Although...'

'What Will?'

'Well I know how much it will pain me to leave Castle Bolton tomorrow morning and it will get worse with each day that we are apart'

'Cheri' she whispered

'Marie I will in someway or another provide for you to come to Hoghton. If approval is not given then it shall be done in secret. Yes!', this last he affirmed by banging his fist on the arm of the sofa.

'Darling Will think no more this evening, we can discuss our plan of action in the morning. Tonight is to enjoy'.

At this exact moment Mary Fleming, her favourite, arrived to enquire if Mary wished to talk or to play cards or chess, but the answer was known even as she spoke for she had seen Mary's companion. 'Thank you Marie' said the queen 'but I have to talk with Master Shakespeare this evening, on a matter of some import' she added, without truly convincing Mistress Fleming that the time was to be spent on discussing affairs of state.

As her companion turned to leave Mary called her back and spoke quietly to her, a few feet away from Will, 'Marie you have always been my confidante in matters of the heart and I suspect you have perceived how happy I have been these past days'. Mary Fleming smiled her answer before her mistress continued 'Could you therefore tell Mary Seton, as delicately as possible, a vous de juger discretion, that I will not be requiring her assistance to prepare for bed this evening.'

Mary Fleming looked towards Will who was now standing over by the fireplace and then she smiled delightedly at Mary, 'Je comprends my lady'. She left the room, calling out cheerily and a little cheekily to Will 'Bonne nuit monsieur '. Will nodded silently.

Mary walked across to him and took his hands in hers 'Now Will, as they say, the night is ours'. Then her coy expression dazzled Will as she pretended to complain 'But unfortunately Mary Seton will not be coming to undress me. How will I manage sir?'

The process was long and slow, beginning as something of a mystery to Will who had never been engaged as a remover of a woman's garments before, but with each complicated layer his incapacity became an irrelevance as Mary took pleasure in helping him, guiding his hands in a series of diversions.

She eventually stood in only her dark blue satin underwear and halted Will, 'Now sir you must explain how I help you, for I have forgotten how to unclothe a man' she lied.

Eventually Will stood naked and Mary raised her arms for him to remove her camisole before sliding down her last remnant. She hugged him close 'Ah Will my fine figure of a man is wanting his woman I feel'. A now no longer self-conscious Will followed her sinuous body towards the bed.

Chapter Twelve

It was almost seven o'clock when Sam and Kate finally arrived back in Leyburn, having enjoyed a leisurely walk back from Castle Bolton, stopping to eat their picnic in the same field where they had made the earlier foodless halt. The journey had been spent in discussion of just what their discovery at Bolton Castle might mean.

They agreed that if Sam's conjecture were true - that Shakespeare had shared a bed with the Catholic Queen of Scotland, then the ramifications were immense. It would seem to confirm indisputably that the Bard was, at least in his younger years, of the same faith as Mary because, as Sam pointed out, 'Passionate woman that she was there's no way she would have had a relationship with one whom she would term 'a heretic' '.

'But Sam do you realise the enormity of all this, the implications? It means that all his texts need to be re-examined for new inferences, for possible plot derivations or inspirations, everything'. Sam was caught up in Kate's enthusiasm.

They headed for the hotel to collect their back-packs but just before they got there Kate stopped, turning Sam round as his hand was pulled back by her. 'Sam'

'What?'

'I'm knackered'

'Which means?'

Kate put on her little-girl-lost expression as she asked 'Do we have to drive over to Hawes tonight? I might not find a place to stay and you'll be late getting home'.

Sam had been wondering how to broach the subject of their having to go separate ways.

'So what do you suggest then Kate?'

'Well I'm hungry now aren't you?'

'Is that morning picnic hungry or afternoon picnic hungry?' he teased her.

She slapped his bottom and laughed suggestively 'Both you bastard if you must know, but one more than the other'. Her thin tee-shirt did nothing to conceal the breasts she provocatively wobbled at him. 'Do you think the hotel would take us back?'

'Is that what you want to do Kate?'

'Don't you?'

'I just want to be with you'

'Why's that Sam?'

'So we can discuss our research of course'

Kate's mood changed briefly to a less flippant one as she looked at him with a straight face and asked 'Joking apart would you be prepared to help me on this Sam?'

'Kate I'm at a loose end writing-wise and you know lass that I'm potty about you'. They kissed.

'C'mon fella, let's ask for the same bed'

'Oh I see *that* hungry'.

She made a grab at the crutch of his shorts but he darted away with a chuckle and ran up to the entrance of the hotel.

Their room was still vacant. 'There you are they must have known us better than we do ourselves' claimed Kate. Sam agreed, though in his mind he was not convinced that she hadn't also had a good idea what they would be doing, the way she had dawdled on the walk back, and if he were totally honest it may also have been a subliminal thought of his own.

'Will you be taking dinner sir?' asked the receptionist

'We're not really hungry yet, maybe later' interceded Kate on Sam's behalf.

They returned to the familiarity of their bedroom. 'Shower?' asked Kate

'Yes sure, you go ahead'

'No we'll spin for it. Heads you soap me first and tails I do you'. She smiled self-satisfiedly. Sam did not argue, he just called 'Heads'.

They shared the shower an hour later.

Dinner was eventually welcomed for they had not eaten a proper meal since the pub-lunch which they ate shortly after they had first met the morning before.

During the meal Sam seemed pensive and Kate put her hand over his and was just about to ask him if he was alright when he looked up, into space rather than her face, and began a speech across the table 'To be or not to be...'

'I think I've heard this one' joked Kate.

Sam only half-smiled, 'Sure, but what's the question Kate? What is Hamlet's dilemma?'

'Well isn't it generally acknowledged that he's in some sort of inner turmoil - about confrontation?'

'Exactly. But stop there!' Kate looked surprised, then he continued 'What if Mr. Shakespeare was echoing his own problem from when he was an adolescent. About confronting the world'

'Not entirely with you yet Sam'

'To declare or not to declare, to come out of the closet or not to, to be open rather than recusant'

'In his catholicism?' she posed 'To be or not to be a catholic?'

'Exactly my beautiful brown-eyed blonde-haired sexy maiden!' Sam's voice rose as he was carried away by his dramatics and this time it was Kate who nervously calmed the adjacent tables with a sympathetic smile.

She turned back to her man 'Oh shit isn't this all so exciting? Just so much to re-explore'. Then she abruptly changed the subject as her face went into tender mode 'I'm in love with you Sam'

'Yes but you only want my brain'

She laughed her dirty laugh again 'That's right, and I really enjoyed the way you used your brain in the shower'

'Kate!' he hushed her as she grinned at him

'Well' she teased 'You know what they say most men think with'

'Shut up woman or I'll smear this trifle on your tits and lick it off right here'

'Great idea. Come on then' and she reached for the top of her strapless dress

'I give up. You out-balls me every time'

'Umm, ironic that' she grinned

As they entered their room Kate, as a precaution against pink-haired invaders, hung the 'Do not disturb' on the door-handle. She flung herself down on the bed. 'Oh Sam isn't life strange, miraculous even. Yesterday morning I was a rather lonely student not knowing exactly where I was going either in my studies or my life. I lose my footing on a hillside and fall into the arms of a man who has wonderfully filled both those gaps'. Sam was quiet, not being used to receiving acclaim of any sort. Kate was still staring at the ceiling as she proclaimed 'The only problem is...' and she kept her serious expression, '...he keeps dragging me off to make love, in fields, in...' but before she could complete her sentence she was smothered as a laughing and protesting Sam dived on top of her.

In the dreamy lull after they had made love Kate stretched out her arm and ran her fingers over Sam's face 'I'm going to miss you like hell after tomorrow fella. Christ I am!'

'Me too Kate. It's all been a bit overwhelming'

'Sam why am I going to Hawes? I was spinning out my days in a way, to fill up the week's holiday'. She paused, then asked 'Would it be awful of me if I asked you to take me all the way home to my cottage tomorrow?'.

Sam was idly fondling her breasts while she spoke. He looked into her dark eyes 'My darling Kate, the more time I spend with you the better. Of course I'll run you home darling'. He kissed her softly

Chapter Thirteen

Will woke up and found himself wrapped in the arms of Mary who was gazing down at him. He realised what the day was about to bring and felt a stab in his stomach. His face displayed his concern to his lover. 'Darling darling Will, today I lose you yes?'

'No Marie, for as you taught me, c'est seulement un au revoir, non un adieu, oui?'

'Oui, mon amour, mais c'est encore difficile, and very painful' she added, as she rolled on top of him. She propped herself up on her arms 'Will since I woke up I have been thinking… I have a plan'. Will blinked himself fully awake as he looked expectantly into her big eyes.

'I told you that from time to time I dress as a man'. Will nodded, 'Every morning that I am to go out riding Jacques, one of my grooms, takes Jupiter for a short hack to warm him up in preparation for my ride. He does this quite early, at about six o'clock. Well, on the day we decide on for my escape I will be Jacques and I will ask Marie Beaton to take my place on Jupiter, she rides adequately and if she covers her face with a veiled cap, as I sometimes do, she will be taken for me, at least for a while. Brackenby never rides closely to me, I do not allow him to'.

Will was excited at this proposal which seemed to be feasible 'And the decoy?' he reminded her.

'Yes I have thought on that too. The evening before, Marie Livingstone will take her evening stroll, which she never misses, and head towards Leyburn. She will take with her one of my shawls'. Will could see what was coming. 'Some little way from here there is an escarpment with bushes growing on it. There she will place my shawl amongst the foliage of a bush'

'So when they find it...'

'They will follow my trail northwards'

'While the following morning you will be riding westwards to me. Oh my clever devious beauty, come here' and Will pulled her down onto his chest and grabbed her tight against him'.

'Oh Will can it work?'

'Marie all we really have in life is hope, hopes for the future, either that things will stay as they are, or improve, depending on one's circumstances. We can only hope my sweetheart queen'

Mary smiled at him but it was a tentative smile in need of reassurance, of confirmation. Then her chameleonesque personality took over as she cast aside her doubts. 'Will do you know that usually, that is when I am alone and not sharing my bed with a young teacher-poet-actor-lover...' she chuckled quietly at her own definition of Will's roles, '...I always eat a boiled egg in bed for breakfast?' Will looked surprised, even moreso after she asked him 'And you sir will you break an egg with me?' Now he was laughing and Mary tried to tickle him as she announced that four eggs were probably being boiled at this very minute 'because I ordered them to be served to us in bed'

So much for royal discretion mused Shakespeare. 'Four?' he queried

'Well young man you have to gather your strength'

'For the journey'

'Well in all truth I was thinking of another activity immediately after the eggs' and Will once more saw that smirk which always affected his loins.

Will had told Mary that on the following Sunday he would have a free day and would request that he be loaned one of Sir Alexander Hoghton's horses in order to improve his riding skills. Before then however he intended to approach Sir Alexander and broach the subject of housing Mary at Hoghton Tower.

It was mid-morning when Mary and Will went to the Nursery to speak with the Maries Beaton and Livingstone who, as always, were readily prepared to risk personal punishment on behalf of their beloved mistress.

Mary, after outlining the plan to her two loyal servants, explained that on the Sunday morning '...although it will mean my foregoing the Holy Mass, I will leave here at six o'clock of the morning'. She was uncertain of the route to Hoghton, having only ever previously ridden as far west as Hawes.

Will promised to meet her there, behind 'The White Bear', '...although you may have to wait awhile Marie for my speed on a horse cannot match yours'

'Well I shall wait until noon but then I will search for a new lover' she teased him. Even this joking stung young Will's tender heart and it showed in his face. 'Oh Will, my darling Will you must know that I am jesting' and she kissed him hard before pushing him away playfully. The two Maries looked embarrassedly at the floor, unused to seeing their queen happily playing with a man.

Fulke arrived anxiously looking for his colleague 'Ah Shakespeare! Excuse me your majesty'. He turned back to Will 'Everyone is kicking their heels, they are ready for the off'

'Two minutes Fulke. In fact start them moving and I will run down the lane to catch you'

'You are coming, yes? You're not staying here for the rest of your life?'

Will glanced at Mary, 'Would that I could Gyllom. Go on, away with you!'

After he had gone Mary asked Will 'Shall you tell Fulke of our plan?'

'Only if Sir Alexander agrees to your coming. If he does not then I will still meet you for I know of a place where we can hide you at Hoghton'

'Oh mon cheri now is the moment. But I praise the Lord that he has found you for me Will, for whereas before I had hoped only to escape, to what life I know not, now I hope to flee to my loved one. Au revoir my darling'. The kiss was long and bitter-sweet. 'I will wave from the same window. A dimanche mon cher '. Will looked once more into her dazzling but sad eyes before he strode away in as brave a manner as he could summon.

Will turned to return Mary's wave as he ran down the lane, causing him to stumble to the ground. He saw her beautiful face with both hands up to her mouth as she laughed with him. He clambered to his feet, dusted himself down, and yelled up at her 'There you are, I've fallen for you!'. Still laughing she blew him a kiss in return.

Will leapt up alongside Fulke and noticed that his friend's eyes were red around the rims, 'Gyllom you've been weeping' he suggested.

'Aye Will, I have left my heart up at the castle'. Then he asked Shakespeare 'but do you not regret losing your queen? You seem not too distressed by your parting'

'Because Fulke I will see her again'.

Gyllom looked at him queringly 'How so sir, you will return here?'

Will sensed immediately that he had already said too much, 'No man, just a gut feeling, an inner sense that something so wonderful cannot have ended today' and turning he looked wistfully back at the receding castle then jumped down from the wagon, 'Time to relieve young Richard from the reins. Cheer up Gyllom, your angel will fly to you again I'm sure'.

When he was left alone Fulke pondered on Will's words and he couldn't help feeling that his poetic colleague had some romantic scheme in his creative head, that he was perhaps plotting to effect a reunion with his royal lover ...*and if so what of my amour, my sweet Angelique? Is she included in Shakespeare's plans?* His ruminating continued until the darkening sky necessitated a search for an overnight stopping place.

Francis Summers in the lead cart suddenly veered off the track towards a copse of trees on slightly higher ground to their left.

After a supper which brought the company back down to earth after the excesses which had been provided at Bolton Castle the boys under the control of Will and Fulke clambered up into their wagons to turn in for the night.

The two friends slowly climbed the escarpment beyond the trees.

'Will'

'Mmm'.

Fulke had learned to recognise this response as a signifier of 'I don't wish to talk', but he proceeded nevertheless, 'Shakespeare what is to become of us?'

Will could not deflect an outright question but he could be obtuse, 'Are we talking of the next five minutes, or lifelong ambitions or...'

'Shut up Shakespeare, you know of what I speak, of the romantic predicaments we have fallen into'

'Ah there's the rub my friend. Did we fall, did we jump or even were we pushed or pulled?'

'You jumped man. The first time you saw her you were lost; whereas I...I bided my time' he added smugly

'Yes, you bided it right until Angelique came to fetch you from your pallias. No Gyllom I think we were both willingly pulled'

'Happen you're right Shakespeare, and my heart is still being tugged'

'We'll think of something Fulke, there will be a way', but Will was worrying what his friend's reaction might be if he were to discover that Mary had escaped to join him but Angelique had been excluded from their scheming. He valued the close bond that he had with Fulke, and would hate to endanger their relationship *...but surely Gyllom must realise that the escape of a monarch has to be a matter of total discretion and secrecy,* although Will immediately acknowledged to himself that such a thought was *...hypocritical pigswill for the truth is I want to be with my lover and the fact that she is a queen matters not one jot. I cannot claim to be freeing a nation's leader, I just want my woman* he admitted. *Anyway it's too* *late now to include the servant-girl. I must confess I didn't know he was so deeply smitten, but how could I?*

All of these conflicting thoughts were still oscillating in young Will's mind as he endeavoured to get to sleep, alone for the first time in three nights. There would follow a day of travelling further away from his beloved Marie, *...no boiled-eggs in bed tomorrow morning.*

Chapter Fourteen

Having assured the hotel-receptionist that they truly would not be returning that evening Sam and Kate wandered through the mid-morning sunshine towards the station.

A parking ticket had been left on the windscreen of Sam's car, 'Oh well I suppose its a small price to pay for an extra day's cultural experience yesterday'

'Is that what it was?' asked a smiling Kate

'Yes, you know the discovery about the bed etcetera'

'Mmmm, a lot of etcetera though Mr. Woodhouse'

'Get in the car woman'

They drove westwards in silence, both wary of discussing their impending separation. They had again missed breakfast so as they entered the outskirts of Hawes Sam suggested that they take a pub-lunch, 'I saw a lovely-looking old pub when I passed through the other day, 'The White Bear' I think it was.

Neither of them had a great appetite but managed a ploughman's each.

'Sam I just can't believe how my life has changed in such a short time; and what a mix of emotions. I'm so excited about what we've discovered and what it means to my academic plans, but even more important than that fella I'm absolutely dotty about you'.

Sam could only look sheepish despite his superior age to this young woman. He remained silent.

'You too eh Sam?'.

He nodded. Then he attempted to lighten the moment, 'Yes I'm really pleased to think that in the middle of her miserable imprisonment Mary maybe found a lover'

Kate was waiting, but his lips stayed closed. 'And?' she prompted.

'Yes there is another emotion...I'm really pissed off about that parking-ticket' and he couldn't contain his laughter before Kate pinched his left thigh under the table.

'Anything else' she queried with her pursed lips suppressing a smile

'Oh yes I forgot, I met the most wonderful girl I've ever known'.

Kate's fingers relaxed as she leant across and kissed him hard. 'Come on lover, I suppose we have to move' and she took his hand as they stood up.

Kate's cottage was just what Sam had been expecting, probably over a hundred years old, with a small front-garden filled with traditional flowers: lupins and snapdragons, margharitas and wallflowers. 'Very Anne Hathaway' he commented as they passed through the little white iron gate and stood on the crazy-paving path.

'Yes' said Kate 'talking of Ms. Hathaway do you think Shakespeare knew Mary before or after, or during his marriage to her?'

'Good question. I don't think there was a great passion between him and Anne was there?'

'Dead right. He had a one-off fling with her in a cornfield when he was eighteen; she got pregnant and some months later two heavy friends of her dead father enforced a shotgun-wedding for young William'

'Wasn't she older than him?'

'Mm Sam you do know a bit about the Bard don't you? Yes she was believed to be twenty-six when they married in November 1582, so eight years older'

'So Shakespeare was only eighteen. I wonder when, that's if, he met Mary'

'No Sam lets be positive, we both believe in them now so let's take that as said. I reckon it could have been anytime during his 'lost years' as they call them. C'mon let's go indoors'

Kate unlocked the oak door to her cottage 'Mind your head Sam, I can't promise I'll give you the kiss of life'.

As she stooped to enter she expected a response to her taunt but Sam was still pondering on Will's marriage, 'Perhaps he did fall for an older woman Kate for that's what we're claiming between him and Mary'

'True'. Kate turned 'But its not that usual for affairs to succeed when there's an age difference is it?' Sam knew he was being teased but her following embrace compensated for that. 'Welcome to my home Samuel', Kate kissed him. 'Come on I'll give you the guided tour, its not quite Bolton Castle though'.

As she passed out of the sitting-room across into the kitchen she continued speaking 'Getting back to Anne Hathaway, academics sometimes claim that Shakespeare indicates his dissatisfaction with the marriage in some of his lines. Like in Twelfth Night, what does Duke Orsino say to Viola? – "Let still the woman take an elder than herself". They walked upstairs. 'Pretty damning of his own predicament wouldn't you say? Then he advises her, who as you know he thinks is a him, "And let thy love be younger than thyself".

'Point taken. Mmm nice big bed, king-size?'

'Yea. I bought it to replace the old divan that was here when I moved in. Bit extravagant really for just me'

'Always just you?' probed Sam

'Yes sir. The other half is unchristened...as yet' she added as she led the way back into the narrow hallway. Sam couldn't see her face.

Kate found some eggs in the 'fridge and offered to cook them omelettes. 'I hope they're still fresh. Oh lets risk it, you need eggs to give you strength'

'For my return journey?'

'Oh Sam don't lets talk of that yet. Its only six o'clock, you can stay awhile can't you?'

Sam flung his arm dramatically into the air as he pronounced 'Until the moon dries up the sea!'

'I don't know that line'

'No Miss Academic, that's because I just invented it for you'

'My darling fella, so you're a writer-lover-poet now!' and she jumped up and wrapped her legs round Sam as he caught her.

They finished off the bottle of Chablis and without any hesitation Kate led Sam up to her bedroom. They began to slowly undress each other and Kate stood in only her black lace panties when there was a loud thumping on the front door.

'Oh shit Sam I know that knock, its David. You stay here, I'll get rid of him'. Then she dashed across into the bathroom for a few seconds before rushing back into the bedroom with dripping hair and flinging on a grey-silk dressing-gown. She turned back and kissed Sam, fondling his balls before dashing out again. Sam just stood amazed at the resourcefulness, and the bravado, of this incredible girl.

He heard the front-door open below. 'Oh David its you. Sorry I took so long I was getting out of the shower. I've only just got home'

'Well *I'm* pleased to see *you*' said David rather pointedly, 'Can I come in?'

'Well...'

The visitor sensed her lack of enthusiasm 'Come on Kate I haven't seen you for over a week. Anyway how did it go? Not too lonely?'

Kate mellowed as she answered 'Absolutely fantastic. I made two marvellous discoveries'. There was a pause, then she continued 'Hang on I'll fetch one of them for you'.

Kate re-entered the bedroom where Sam had put his jeans back on. She pulled open her dressing-gown to flash herself at him, 'Come on my man I want you to meet someone'

'Kate!'

'Sam he's got to know about us. I want the whole world to know. I'm proud of you'

Sam could have thrown her on the bed right now he felt so elated at these words. 'So I'm not to be your guilty secret then?'

'No way fella. Come on' and she tugged him towards the door.

David heard the padding of bare feet descending the stairs and saw four legs appear which became Kate and a man of about forty dressed in only a pair of black jeans. Sam saw a curly-headed gaunt-looking young man, maybe mid-twenties, whose glaring eyes were oscillating between his hand, still clasped by Kate, and his bare chest.

'David this is Sam. We met near Castle Bolton and he has agreed to help me with my research. He's an expert on the Stuarts'.

The youth remained silent, then, glowering, spoke slowly and curtly to Kate 'I see, and does this joint research have to be done upstairs and semi-naked then?'

Kate was not feeling in a patient mood, 'No David it doesn't. Sam is dressed like this because of his other role in my life. When you knocked we were about to start shagging'

'What! You cow you know how much I think of you'

'How many times have I told you we can only ever be mates'

'Fuck mates!' - he slammed the door as he left.

Sam looked incredulously at Kate before bursting into a smile, 'Oh Kate why didn't you give it to him straight lass?'

Laughing she threw herself down onto the sofa and opened her gown. 'You mean we should have done it in front of him? Come on then my horny hunk, lets start here in case he comes back'

'You are one wicked woman'. Sam felt her unbuckling his belt

'A shrew?' she giggled.

The ringing of Sam's mobile woke them up. The sun was streaming through the little panelled windows. 'Sam this is Mike. Where the hell are you? We had an appointment for ten o'clock this morning'

'Oh shit Mike, sorry! Look I'm over in Lancashire. Can I see you this afternoon, about three?'. He switched off his phone and turned to the big brown eyes that were looking up at him puzzledly. 'My agent. I totally forgot I'd arranged to meet him. It must be Monday'.

Kate sat up and kissed him softly, 'Who's been playing truant then Samuel?'. She beamed as she then asked him 'And who's been sleeping in my bed? A big bare man I think'. She adopted a pensive look 'Three o'clock where?'

'Darlington'

'Darlington, say two hours drive at the most. Mmm plenty of time for breakfast in bed I'd say'.

Chapter Fifteen

Will sat staring silently into his pint of ale. He was deep in thought but his demeanour could have signified another mood, that which Fulke interpreted it as.

'Shakespeare fellow why so miserable? Come on lad its Saturday night and tomorrow we have free'. Will looked up at him blankly, his friend continued 'Look fellow I know you're missing her but you have to try and forget Mary'

'Its that easy is it Gyllom?'

'It could be tonight' and he felt a nudge in his ribs, 'Have you seen Alice behind the bar? Her dumplings are fair bubbling out of that frock. Its her birthday and we are invited to her party later. You know what she thinks of you' Fulke leered.

Still Will looked impassive. He longed to share his thoughts with his dear mate, to tell him of how what he had thought to be a simple plan to be re-united with his beloved Marie had just become complicated. He wanted to tell Fulke of his conversation with Sir Alexander Hoghton:

'Shakespeare I am impressed by your noble intentions, your determination to free the Catholic Queen, but I cannot be any part of it. Only last week, during your absence, we were visited by officers representing the Privy Council. They warned me that it is known that we celebrate Mass here and that future violations of Queen Elizabeth's directive against such practice will be harshly punished. I cannot allow the Queen of Scots to hide here with such threats hanging over me'

'But sir'

'Shakespeare no! However...' and the lord's voice lowered despite there being no-one else in the chamber 'if you wish to harbour her unbeknown to me you might find some secret place'. Will's face lightened. 'But I must insist that if ever she were discovered on my premises it will be your neck on the block. I hope I speak figuratively but in these times even that could become literal'

'Thank you my Lord'

'Shakespeare tell me one thing, I sense that your enthusiasm to help this woman is more than an act of loyalty to a monarch. Take care young man that the loss of your heart does not lead to that of your head'

'Sir, if pressed I have to confess that I am fair smitten by Marie'

'Marie eh? Mmm. Shakespeare that is all, unless you have anything to add'

'Well' and Will hesitated, 'I was wondering sir if on Sunday I might use one of your horses. I went riding with Queen Mary whilst we were waiting for the repair of our cart and I would dearly love to improve my technique'

'And would such equestrian practice involve your heading eastwards sir? No, do not answer that. I am to remain ignorant of your actions. Remember my boy that any rescue attempt is only of your doing'

'Thank you kindly sir'

Will had subsequently visited Davey, Sir Alexander's head-groom, and persuaded him, with a little financial incentive, to prepare one of his better steeds for five o'clock on Sunday morning. He had to be very careful but he explained that he might be returning with another acquisition for Lord Hoghton's stable.

Will's musing was interrupted as the birthday girl arrived at their table, looking provocative in her new pale blue dress with its amply filled scoop-necked bodice. As she sat down she flung an arm across his shoulders. 'Willie why so glum? I've been watching you all night. Are you not pleased to see Alice after your week away?'

Shakespeare smiled weakly 'Surely Alice'.

She remained unconvinced and she nudged her right breast against his arm 'Well I've missed you lad, you know I'm right fond of you'. She spoke sharply across to Fulke 'Do you not have to relieve yourself Gyllom?'

Will regretted the departure of his colleague, leaving him to this slaughtering lamb who whispered into his ear 'You realise I'm sixteen today'

'Congratulations Alice. Happy birthday indeed' he added half-heartedly.

'Sixteen Willie. Sixteen and legal, so I'll come back for you when we close'. She winked as she got up to leave, making the most of the manoeuvre to give him more than a glimpse of her attributes which belied her tender years.

Shakespeare felt his life was suddenly becoming too complicated for one so young, *A week ago I was a virgin and now I am being offered a second bed-partner within days.*

Fulke returned grinning apishly, 'What did Alice want, or do I not need to know?' It seemed to be the night for winks and nudges. 'She's sixteen isn't she Shakespeare?' His tone was mocking in its inquisitiveness.

'Yes'

'Sixteen and ripe as a pear, or as a pair eh?'. Fulke laughed at his own bawdy pun. He knew he could be frank with his closest friend 'And are you going to bed her then?'

Will looked horrified 'Fulke! What do you think I am man? You know I am in love'

'Yes but Mary is now lost to you. The queen is dead long live.... Oops sorry Shakespeare!'

Will turned sharply to his friend, whose smile was undiminished as he continued 'Well in that case Shakespeare I may offer myself to Alice as a substitute'

'For Christ's sake Gyllom, what of Angelique? How can you be so fickle? You were destroyed when we left Bolton'

'But that was four days ago man. The queen is...oh shut up Gyllom' and he slapped his own thigh gleefully.

Will, amidst his disgust at his friend's shallowness, was also relieved, for such an attitude could mean that his own worries about not arranging Angelique's escape might be unnecessary.

'Seriously Will are you to refuse young Alice?'. There was a hopeful tone to Gyllom's voice.

Shakespeare didn't answer but got to his feet and looked down at his friend, 'Fulke I'm off, I'm rising at five tomorrow morning. I intend to go riding for the day. Feel free if you are so inclined. I will see you tomorrow evening', with which he stood up and left a gawping friend speechless. He felt a pair of deep blue eyes at the bar following him out of the tavern.

Will was really worried now; he had been riding for most of the morning but had only just reached the Yorkshire Moors. His horse was tiring and he was absolutely exhausted, never having ridden for such a period before. He knew he should stop soon but was also conscious that Mary, who was an expert horsewoman, would have travelled the shorter distance to Hawes in barely more than an hour. She would now be fretting that having to wait several hours for Will she was running the risk of re-capture. He was terrified as it occurred to him that even at this moment she might be being taken back to her prison, depending on how much time her captors had spent on following the false trail northwards. He realised that too little thought had been given to the planning of their respective rides.

Will had almost reconciled himself to the fact that his foolhardy plan had failed and that he now stood little chance of ever again seeing his adored Marie. He had now slowed his mount to a walk, having just trotted through Horton-in-Ribblesdale. Suddenly he heard a whooping noise from the spinney halfway up the escarpment to his left and he saw a young man urging his horse down the precarious slope. Will froze. Could this be one of Knowles' men who had been lying in wait to arrest him as an accomplice of the Scottish Queen? The rider skidded to a halt, his face masked by a scarf and the overhang of his velvet cap. There came no words of arrest but nevertheless Will decided to act the innocent. He greeted the newcomer in a casual manner 'Good morrow sir. I see we share the same moor, have you travelled far?'

'Not far enough my fellow for I ride to meet my loved one to the west'

'Why there's a thing, I too am on such a mission'. Will realised as soon as he had spoken that this was a stupid confession to make.

The man was now studying his face closely then he leaned across towards him, 'I have to tell you sir that I am also attracted by a young man such as yourself. Would you consider lying with me awhile in this lush grass?'

Will's face reddened and he bore an expression of horrified disgust 'Away with you fellow, I am not of that ilk'

'Well I shall lie right here. I leave you to your conscience' and with that the man jumped agilely down from his horse, sat on the grass and flung off the cap, bursting into laughter as a cascade of chestnut hair tumbled down'

'Marie! How can you tease me so?'

'Oh Will you were wonderful. You should have seen your face when I played you for a queer-boy'

Shakespeare slid off his mount and threw himself beside Mary, attempting to bury his head on her constricted bosom. His lover stroked his hair. 'Are you not pleased to see me Master Shakespeare?'

'Oh God Marie I love you so'.

As Mary lifted his head she saw tears trickling. 'I'm sorry Will', she was still grinning, 'but I could not stay too long in Hawes for I was too soon arrived. After an hour or so I rode westwards as far as the crossroads just to the north of here. I was not certain from which direction you would be coming so I rode to the summit of that fell, from where I could watch both roads' and she pointed up beyond the spinney. Will was still in shock as he gazed at the movement of her beautiful lips. 'I saw you approaching some time since and rode down into the copse of trees'. Mary's voice changed to a calmer and mellower tone 'Come Will you have not kissed me yet'.

The request was granted at length until Mary broke away, 'I see sir that your ardour has not softened during our absence' and she reached down to confirm her suspicion. 'There is taller grass yonder my man. Do you think a queen has lain in such a royal bed before?'

Their lovemaking was tender, despite almost a week of mutual longing, for their mood of relief at being finally reunited demanded a slowly savoured celebration.

The sun blazed down on this incongruous couple, Mary presenting a strangely ambiguous figure with her manly riding-breeches now pulled up again but with her breasts still absorbing the warm rays. 'Oh William would that we could just lie here forever. That is all I would ask of life mon cheri - away from all politics, intrigue and jealousies'. She turned her head from the sky to look into his eyes 'You are a silent one today Will. Are you still shocked by my surprise?'.

He answered slowly 'My only shock my darling Marie is in realising that we have actually succeeded in re-meeting. My heart has filled my mouth too much to speak'.

Mary rolled on top of him and kissed him softly but Will couldn't hide a wince of pain which caused her to look alarmed, 'Mais mon cher qu'est-ce que c'est?', Will looked puzzled. 'I'm sorry darling, what is it?'

Now he looked embarrassed as he confessed 'It's my rear'.

Mary rolled off him and turned him over 'Mon Dieu! Poor Will you are like a baboon! This is your first long ride yes?' He nodded as her gentle hands tenderly felt his bottom. 'Will it is impossible for you to ride all the way back to Hoghton this afternoon. Oh my darling what can we do? We must find a place for the night. How far since you passed through a village?'

Will looked concerned 'Well Horton, another Horton, is but three or four miles back, but is it not risky to be seen in public?'

Mary leaped to her feet and, lowering her voice by an octave asked 'And what is risky about two young male travellers spending a night at an inn together?' Will had to laugh as she promised 'I undertake not to share your bed if you wish it so sir'.

They dressed themselves, Will smiling as his beautiful woman de-feminised herself by tightly binding her breasts into a proud masculine chest which she thrust out at him. 'Do I still take your fancy William?'.

His answer was to firmly grasp her buttocks as he pulled her to him and smilingly whisper 'Why sir you could turn a man from the straight and narrow'.

Mary giggled as she helped him to tentatively climb back onto his horse. Will looked serious 'I am fearful that I will be missed this evening at Hoghton, but only Fulke knows of my absence and he will surely cover for me. Yes, then we must rise very early tomorrow morning and make our way there. We could arrive by nine o'clock'

He saw the return of his lover's sexy grin as she suggested 'If we must rise so early it may not be worth sleeping at all tonight, but we must to our beds as soon as we arrive'.

Chapter Sixteen

'Look Sam it's been almost two years since you wrote anything, I've got both of your publishers leaning on me'. Sam's agent Mike wore such a pleading expression on his well-fed face.

'Two years?'

'Two years Samuel. In fact you've written nothing since your split with Sally. She didn't take all your pens with her did she?'

Sam smiled to himself as it occurred to him that perhaps now he had been 're-mused'. 'Mike I wasn't looking forward to this meeting when we arranged it, I'd got no ideas, but now I think I may have something germinating'

'Well get the fertiliser out man, I have to live off you you know! Anyway what is this something?'

'The Scottish Queen'

'Yea? Shit Sam I think you're in love with that woman, there's no future in it you know. I hope it's a new angle, there are loads of books on her around' and he distractedly shuffled two pens on his desk as he spoke.

'Mike this could be dynamite. You know I went hiking last week, well I met someone, also into history as it happens. We got on brilliantly and spent a few days together'

'Sounds like fun, two middle-aged fogies talking of the past'. Mike feigned a wide yawn.

Sam could not suppress his laugh of reaction, 'Not exactly a fogy Mike - twenty-three, tall, blonde and very very female'

Now he sat up. 'You randy old sod. Well good luck to you if she makes your ink flow'

'She surely does that'

'No Sam' and the agent was grinning now 'I'm talking literal here not metaphor. Anyway what's this TNT.?'

'I'm not being awkward Mike but at the moment I'd really rather not say too much about it. Just leave me to it. Another thing is that Kate, my fogey, is working with me but on a different part of our jigsaw'

'So that's how you spent your time together, have you finished the edge pieces yet?'

'Shut up and listen. It sort of involves two extremely important figures from history; my half is Mary Stuart and Kate is doing her Ph.D. on the other one'

'Who is?' the agent's eyebrows raised in anticipation

'Sorry Mike I can't tell you. I have to respect Kate's confidence too and I'm sure she wouldn't want me to spread her theory around just yet. In fact I feel a bit guilty that I've even told you about my idea I'll have to discuss it with her'

'Would Kate happen to live in Lancashire?'

'Mm'

'And would Kate perhaps be the reason that you missed our appointment this morning?'

'Shit Mike you always manage to make me feel like a guilty schoolboy'

Mike slapped him on the back as they stood up, 'Only teasing Mike. Now get out of here and put your pen to work, but not too much at your age'

'Bastard!' They shook hands.

Sam phoned Kate in the evening and told her of his idea that they could write a book together and of his conversation with Mike.

She was delighted to be acknowledged as his inspirational influence and was excited that he saw a piece of work of his own arising out of their joint research. 'So we can spin off each other' he added

'That would be brilliant; my name first on the cover though' she teased. Sam ignored her flippancy.

'Kate I'm going down to London tomorrow, I want to spend a few days in the British Library'

'Ok my darling. I'll ring you tomorrow night on your mobile. Sleep well'

'Sleep lonely'

'I know' Kate sighed.

Two days later Sam rang the bell for a second time but still there was no reply, then from around the corner leading to the back of the cottage there appeared a figure dressed in a donkey-jacket, scruffy denims and a woolly hat. The apparition shuffled forward, head bowed and addressed him in a gruff voice 'Hiya mate, seen the lady of the house? I'm expecting a hot weekend here'.

Sam would recognise those gorgeous brown eyes anywhere, he played along 'Sorry guv, but I fancy you meself. Get your kecks off Kate before you turn me gay!'

She tugged off her hat, letting her golden bob fall free, 'Well Sam you sounded so excited on the phone last night about your discovery that Mary was into cross-dressing so I thought I'd better try and turn you on'. She walked up and wrapped her arms around him 'Hey fella give your woman a kiss in the margaritas' and she jumped into the flower bed.

'I'll stick with your lips in public if you don't mind. Your daisies will have to wait till we're indoors'

They stooped through the front door into the sitting-room. 'God Sam I've missed you like crazy' She hugged him tightly. 'You must be tired after your journey back'

'You can't get me into bed that easy young lady. Anyway I smell cooking'

'I see, four nights away and your stomach has become your primary organ'

'Right that's it! I can't play it cool any longer' and he chased her round the room and slipped off her donkey-jacket to discover that she was wearing nothing underneath, nor beneath her jeans.

'I thought perhaps you might be in a hurry' Kate laughingly explained, then she lifted her arms above her head and danced gracefully around the sofa before spreading herself down on it.

'Christ Sam that was good, I'll have to dress up more often'

'I think madam it had nothing to do with your being a roadworker. But anyway don't you think it's interesting about the cross-dressing?'

'Course! Look at the times Shakespeare had female characters doing it in his plays - Portia, Viola, Rosalind and who was that in *Two Gentlemen of Verona*? Helen that's it'

'So you think your man could have been influenced by Mary doing it?'

'Well it's certainly an argument isn't it? They always claim that the only way women could be given powerful roles in his plays was to pretend that they were men. Portia was just an object for her suitors wasn't she but when she slipped into the lawyer's gear hey - she turned Shylock over, lost him his Sunday-joint, and saved Bassanio's life'

They were still talking as they wandered naked into the kitchen where Kate pulled a lasagne out of the oven. 'Hope this isn't ruined'

'But Kate, Mary didn't need to attain power, she was a queen'

'No Sam that's not what I'm saying. It's just that Shakespeare may have got the idea from seeing Mary, who had once had power, dressed like a bloke'. They sat down to eat and Kate was well into her theory now, 'Ordinary women, non-monarchs if you like, were decidedly the second sex, unvoiced, but Shakespeare, in a mode of carnivalesque topsy-turvy, inverted the norms. This appealed to half of his audience of course. Probably started a whole different way of considering the family unit in some homes'. Kate was now the excited academic.

'Will the feminist. Took a few hundred years to happen though didn't it?' Sam offered.

'Yes because even in the plays it wasn't allowed to last, carnival doesn't does it? Viola for instance in *Twelfth Night* - ok she was influential as the lad Cesario but as soon as she was revealed as a woman and betrothed to Orsino we never hear a word out of her'

'Point taken. Hey Kate this lasagne's great. So you cook as well as you...'.

He stopped himself as they both burst out laughing and Kate told him 'That's enough poetry man, come on' and she led him from the table.

Chapter Seventeen

Four hundred years later the landlord of the inn at Horton-in-Ribblesdale, whose antecedents had been blissfully unaware of who the pair of overnight guests were and would feel no compulsion to erect a blue plaque proclaiming that 'William Shakespeare and Mary Queen of Scots slept here - together!'

The two anonymous travellers were not fondly remembered at the time for one of them, perhaps a poet or a balladeer, had borrowed a quill and ink and scribbled some graffiti on the bedroom wall, something like 'There was a lover and his lass' and some other nonsense like 'with a hey-ho and a hey-nonny-no'. It had taken the maid, Marianne, several hours to completely remove it. Then there was a missing cushion. This would have been found nestling in the back of Will's breeches as a palliative against the painful ride.

Will and Mary did sleep there however, if only for two or three hours, for their respective appetites of youth and reawakening required many hours to be sated. They had paid for the room when they arrived, explaining to their host that they needed to make an early start the following morning.

The landlord could confirm that they had left shortly after five o'clock for he was woken by the rattling of horses' hooves beneath his window at that hour.

They turned the tree-shrouded corner, rode through the lodge gates and halted, for Mary was impressed by the view before them. Hoghton Tower stood majestically on the brow of a hill, some half-mile or more distant and between them and it the approach track dropped initially into a wood-lined valley before ascending to the walled home of Sir Alexander Hoghton.

Nudging their mounts the couple trotted on and had just reached the bottom of the slope when a rider emerged from the trees. He seemed aged and weak in the way he leaned forward over his mount's neck. Mary tensed up as she feared the worst but was relieved as the rider slowly dismounted and dropped awkwardly to his knees beside her. He spoke in a quavering voice that echoed his physical state, 'Your majesty, Sir Alexander Hoghton at your service'.

Mary smiled to herself for Will had already explained to her the limited conditions of such service. She offered her hand and addressed the heavily coated figure 'Sir I thank you for your offer of hospitality, but is my disguise so transparent?'

Sir Alexander was now standing 'Why indeed not your majesty, but when Shakespeare had not returned yesterday evening I concluded that he must have ridden to you at Castle Bolton and then found the return journey impossible to attempt'. Mary did not respond. Hoghton continued 'I hope that your highness will find your stay here amenable'.

Now she quickly interceded 'Well I would sir if I were indeed here' and raising her eyebrows she smiled at his employer in a manner which Will saw as being distinctly superior but also an attempt to charm.

Sir Alexander swept his hat across his knees and remounted, 'I bid you good day your majesty for I must continue on my medicinal ride. I regret I am not in the best of health these days'. Mary nodded her acknowledgement before she and Will rode on.

Shakespeare's original plan, if they had arrived under cover of darkness the night before, had been to secrete Mary in one of the small cell-like storage rooms beneath the kitchens but now their arrival would be more evident and therefore, in view of Mary's effective disguise, they decided to brave it out and take breakfast which was still being served in the Smoking Room off the King's Hall.

Will was immediately surrounded by welcoming colleagues as they entered. He presented Mary as Stewart, a lad who had discovered his prone body after he had fallen from his horse yesterday afternoon. Will told how, since he had been unable to continue riding, the two of them had rested overnight in a nearby tavern. Stewart would be leaving after he had taken breakfast, for he had kindly accompanied him to Hoghton only to ensure that Will returned home safely.

The story was accepted but, after sitting down together at a separate table, Will tightened up as he saw the approach of the Hoghton gossip, the aptly named Robert 'Hugh' Jemouth, a foppishly-dressed youth who dramatically raised his hands as he spoke 'Shakespeare good to see you. So who is your handsome companion?'

'Jemouth I present Mister McQueen, my rescuer of yesterday'. Mary offered her hand in greeting whilst Will hoped that 'Hugh' would not find it odd that a fellow would have such elegantly long and soft fingers, but the youth was too full of his own news to notice,

'Have you heard about Gyllom? Yesterday morning we all thought the two of you had decided to leave Hoghton for some reason, for nobody had seen either of you since Saturday evening in the Red Lion'. Will frowned in puzzlement as Jemouth went on 'Then the Taylor youth remembered that shortly before he left the tavern he had seen Fulke sitting with Alice, you know, the barmaid. They were kissing and fondling each other. We think he has spent all of the weekend with her, for the room which the two of you share was empty last night. What do you think of that eh Will?'.

Having accomplished his muck-spreading Jemouth stood up and left, doubtless to inform all others of who the new fellow was.

Mary gazed at Will and she was looking very upset, 'Will how can this be? Fulke! Does he not realise that there is the sweetest girl at Castle Bolton who is desperately pining for him? She was so distraught that I felt truly guilty that I could not offer to bring her along with me'.

Will looked embarrassed, but on his friend's behalf. He felt unable to offer an explanation for Fulke's fickleness.

'Oh ma pauvre Angelique!'. Mary put her face in her hands, perhaps too feminine a gesture in the circumstances.

He tried, albeit weakly, to justify Gyllom's behaviour, 'Marie I know that Fulke felt deeply for Angelique, but he also thought never to see her again after we left Castle Bolton, for I kept our plans secret from him. Was that wrong of me?'

Mary lifted her head, composed now 'No my darling it was not, it was the only way. Anyway it would have been impossible for her to accompany us, not least because the disappearance of both she and me would have offered only one conclusion, that we had both fled to our lovers of the week before'. Mary at this moment longed to embrace her Will but she had to restrain herself from even placing her hand on his.

They sat waiting until the room emptied before Will led Mary out and across the Inner Courtyard, past the Great Hall, to the archway in the far corner which led to the kitchens. Will looked into the hallway fronting the first room and seeing no-one near the doorway he signalled Mary to follow him. They turned left and descended the stairway into a dark underground passage, walking along to the point where it turned an angle to the right. Off of this corner was the largest of the rooms, one piled high with sacks of flour.

'Marie I'm sorry but at the moment I can offer you only this poor home but I promise to speak with Sir Alexander again'

Mary took his hand and squeezed it 'Fear not Will, I would sleep in a midden if it meant I could be near you'. They stood in the whitened room and kissed long and passionately.

Gasping, Will told her 'I will obtain a mattress from the maids and bring it down here as soon as I can'

'What will you have to do for such a favour sir? I trust it will not require a testing of the bed before she gives it to you'

'Marie!

'Ah poor Will, you still haven't learned how I tease have you mon cher? Oh and darling do you think there might be a change of clothing available? I cannot live as a man forever or I may start looking at the maids myself' – again that sexy upturned grin.

'Surely ma belle. I will undress the donor myself', Shakespeare kept his face straight.

'That's better William. You are learning' she laughed.

It was not until lunchtime that Will met up with Fulke, when he came to sit by him at the communal table.

'Did you miss me these past two nights Will? I'm afraid I was detained at a young lady's pleasure'. The expected response of an encouraging nudge between two jack-the-lads was not forthcoming. 'What's up Shakespeare? Something is bothering you. Do you wish you *had* taken up Alice's offer? Hey you're jealous man are you not?'

The bait was not taken up. 'Fulke we have to talk, let's go outside'.

The two companions, both frowning, one with worry and the other with incomprehension, walked across the Inner Courtyard, through the Upper Gateway and down the few steps into the deserted Lower Courtyard.

'What is it Will? You look terrible'

Shakespeare had been pondering on this moment for a week now. Still looking perturbed he looked at his friend, 'Fulke I wasn't here either last night'. Gyllom's frown returned. 'You see... look...you know I told you I was going riding yesterday'

'Yes you said so in the Lion'

'Well I rode off to meet someone. Fulke you must swear never, under any circumstances or pressures, to repeat what I am telling you now. I still think it might be better for you if you didn't know, but as soul-mates we have always shared everything yes?'

'Will you're worrying me. What's up fellow?'

He blurted it out 'Marie is here!'

'Jesus Christ and Mother Mary!' Now Gyllom's own frown turned to one of concern 'Is she alone?'

'That's what I was so upset about, not telling you of our plan during the week Fulke. We had to leave Angelique at Bolton Castle'

'Gads Will! Thank the Lord you did' and he mock-wiped his brow.

'What?'

'Alice man. I'm thinking of marrying her. Can you imagine if Angelique were to suddenly arrive?'

'Oh Fulke you're as mad as I am'

'Steady on Shakespeare I wouldn't agree there. But where is Mary? Does Sir Alexander know? Is she staying? You mean she's escaped?'

'Slowly, slowly my friend. She is here without his lordship officially knowing. I have hidden her somewhere and he is not to know where. Now promise me Fulke you will keep this to yourself'

'On my honour' and he slapped Will on the shoulder

'Mmm, that's what bothers me'. This comment restored their relationship to normal as the two of them wrestled a mock fight on the cobbles, rolling over and over. Suddenly Fulke stopped his brawling. 'Will I've thought of something. Alice wants me to spend every night in the village, in her room, but I cannot keep doing that. I would have to get up at dawn to arrive here on time, I was late this morning. I have promised her one more night and then she must wait until Saturday, so...' and he slapped his mate on the back as they clambered to their feet 'so there will be a spare bed in our room tonight'

Will had passed from troubled abjection to delighted joy during this conversation with his close friend. 'Whatever becomes of us in life Gyllom I will never forget these times' and he hugged his dear friend warmly.

'Shut up Shakespeare or you'll have me weeping like a woman. Come on lover-lad we have pupils to teach'

'You go on Fulke, I'm free for an hour yet'.

Gyllom waved over his shoulder as he ran up the steps.

Will waited until his friend had passed out of sight before turning into the kitchen-building and going down to see Mary. He was surprised to find the door slightly ajar. He stepped inside warily. There was a small skylight high on the wall of the room but in the gloom he couldn't see her as he closed the door behind him. 'Marie' he whispered. Silence. He called again, louder, but no response came. Now he was worried; he returned to the doorway and peered out. Will froze as he saw white powdery footprints of flour leading down the corridor. He flushed with panic and uttered an oath then, frowning, spoke aloud to himself 'It looks that Fulke may have been right. Has she gone, abandoned me now that I've got her away from Bolton Castle? Oh cursed woman!' and he fell to his knees, banging his fists on the stone floor.

He remained on all fours for several minutes then he froze as a hand tapped him on his shoulder. Fearing the worst, expecting to find an angry Sir Alexander, or even Elizabeth's men, he turned slowly round to look up at a tall slender figure with the body of a man but a face containing two bleary but still beautiful hazel eyes. 'My God Marie!' he blurted out as he leapt to his feet and hugged her. 'You were not in the room'.

'Oui William I was' she tenderly assured him, stroking his eyes. 'Come I will show you where I must have dropped off to sleep'. The queen took his hand and led him back through the door and round behind the piles of sacks to where she had resourcefully made herself an armchair out of the bags of flour. 'My dearest where did you think I was?'

'Marie I found the door open, your tracks on the stones…' he forced back the tears.

'Yes my love, you were a long time gone so I wandered out there to see if you were coming, but then I realised the danger so I returned here and sat to await you. Oh Will you look terrible'.

Shakespeare admonished himself for doubting her loyalty. He put on a brave face and, looking around, changed the subject, adopting a censorious tone to mask his inner turmoil 'Oh my darling you seem more a prisoner now than ever you did at Bolton. Something must be changed. I won't have this for a queen!' he shouted.

'Will that is the first time I have seen you angry, but do not fret my love. Look I can reach out and touch you now – something that I bethought never to be able to do again when you left Castle Bolton'.

Will sat at her feet and felt her sensuous hands combing through his hair. 'Marie I have seen Fulke'. He paused. 'I have told him of your presence here. He has sworn to tell no-one' he reassured her.

'And what of the barmaid, Alice was it?'

'He claims to be betrothed to her'

'But no! I would say he is too young but then I was only fifteen years of age when I married my poor little Francis in Paris'

'The Dauphin?'

'Oui, a grand ceremony in that gloomy Notre Dame'. Mary's wistful expression lightened, 'But he was no virile and lusty young lover such as I have now'. Her spirits in this dark cell were undiminished as she smiled broadly and rose to her feet. 'I really must get out of this manly clothing William and this binding cramps me so. Would you help me sir?' and she began to undress.

'Ooh young man I fear your leggings are becoming too tight for you now' and she giggled as she reached out and grasped him.

The young students gasped then tittered as their tutor entered the room. He looked truly ghostlike with white streaks in his hair and a pale-powdered face.

Chapter Eighteen

Sam sat up in bed as the naked waitress brought him a tray of fragrant coffee, croissants, orange juice and hot buttered toast.

'Umm one could get used to this lifestyle' he mused aloud. 'I particularly like the staff's uniform'

'Well don't get too used to it my dear because you will be the staff tomorrow morning' and Kate waggled her breasts at him as she placed the tray on his lap. 'Balance that if you can' she taunted before clambering in beside him.

Kate was now in academic mode. 'Sam What do you think about a trip to Hoghton Tower? We could drive there in twenty-five, thirty minutes'

'Sounds brilliant, probably nothing on Mary there, but I'd love to. Anything to escape my siren' he laughed as he threw her off him, slapped her bottom and dashed for the shower.

Kate gave out her dirty laugh when she heard his muffled voice call out 'And I want a lock putting on the inside of this cubicle'. Then she quickly leaped out of bed and ran to join him. Under the hot water she shouted 'I take it that was your roundabout way of an invitation eh Sam?'

During the drive to Hoghton Sam and Kate returned to the topic of their now jointly accepted belief that Shakespeare and Mary Queen of Scots had effected a liaison at Bolton Castle.

'Liaison Sam! Is that what we've done 'effected a liaison'? They were lovers weren't they? I hope you don't go carving the initials of every girl you liaise with'

'It's a good job you're driving or someone would be being spanked right now' he laughed.

'But Sam how long do you think they knew each other, because if I'm to argue that his works indicate an effect which she had on him, he's not going to be greatly influenced by a one-night fling in a Flemish bed is he?'

'True. And if they did maintain a relationship, how? I mean yes maybe he met Mary when the Hoghton players took a play there or something, but he would have had to return to Lancashire afterwards'

'Mmm...Sam you've perhaps got something. Look I know this might sound ridiculous, but all of our conjectures are going to involve a bit of gambling with ideas. I am already bored with the university research machine whereby everybody regurgitates someone else's writing. All a bit incestuous I always feel. I think we should be going out on a limb about this. Oh look we're in the village, we have to turn right into that driveway'.

Kate drove slowly up the long tree-lined incline to Hoghton Tower.

As she parked the car she turned to Sam and continued 'We know there were supposed to have been several escape attempts made by Mary, the 'Leyburn Shawl' for instance. What if one of them was successful and she came...'

'Here?'

'Why not? It's here where Shakespeare was and if they were in love where else would she want to be?'

'Shit Kate this is incredible. I feel we're like a couple of detectives'. He kept a straight face as he put his arm round her and announced 'In fact you have a bit of the look of Miss Marple'

'You cheeky sod. Right you'll pay for that later' she smiled, as he ran off towards the entrance.

They wandered around Hoghton Tower, not truly a building large enough to call a stately home, but with an interesting ambience to it, particularly for Kate and Sam whose beliefs or suspicions could never be guessed at by the handful of other visitors present.

As they sat in the Rose Garden Sam asked 'Well?'

'Yes. I've seen the place before as you know, when I came to the 'Lancastrian Shakespeare' conference here, but, oh I don't know. I mean if Mary was here I think she would have had to be in hiding because the Hoghtons, like every other Catholic family at the time, would have been subjected to periodic raids by Queen Elizabeth's 'trouble-shooters' for want of a better word. We haven't seen all the rooms I know but I don't think she would have stayed in what are now the family's private quarters do you Sam?'

'I agree. The only place we haven't been, and which intrigues me, is beyond that 'no entry' rope in the Kitchen Building. I would like to look around there. It seemed like there was a staircase going down at the end of the corridor.'

'We could perhaps ask the owners if we may have a peek. Tell them we're doing research etcetera'

'Bit cheeky'

'Well' and Kate suddenly smiled faintly as she recalled 'In a way I sort of know Lady Rosanna'

'How come?'

'One afternoon during that conference I was with three colleagues from uni, plus John, a guy who had been a mature student. He was even older than you Sam'

'That old?'

'Yes but fun. Anyway we were sitting on a wall, over there in fact, when we saw this very elegant woman arrive and ask a family who were wandering round if they were members of the public. When they said yes she politely asked them if they could come back the next week because the place was shut for a conference. John, who would speak to anyone, got talking to her and asked where she was from. She told him Italy and he lives there now so they chatted about that. Then he asked her if she worked at Hoghton Tower, thinking she was a P.A. or something'

'And'

Kate laughed, 'She said "Well actually I am Lady Rosanna, the owner".'

'Oh shit!'

'Yes but John wasn't at all fazed. We all creased up but he just carried on talking to her. So as you see in a way she and I have met'

'Come on then lass, let's see if we can find her to ask permission'

'Right. Oh Sam I'm sure this is all leading somewhere, it's exciting isn't it?' and she gave a little jump like a schoolgirl.

The Florentine Lady Rosanna, after receiving a message via the ticket office and her private secretary that a delegate from last year's conference would like to see her, agreed to speak with Kate and Sam. Strikingly dressed in a scarlet suit and with her jet-black hair stylishly coiffured she smiled with them as she recalled John's faux pas. 'I remember remarking to an American friend who was with me at the time that in fact I do work here, probably as hard as anyone'.

Kate confided to her their perhaps outlandish theory that Mary Queen of Scots had hidden out at Hoghton Tower to be with the young Shakespeare.

'What a wonderfully romantic idea. I would love to be able to confirm it my dears, as we Italians say 'magari!' - 'I wish!'. However, I became very involved myself in the preparations and some of the research for the conference and I can assure you that there is no record of Mary being even a visitor here'.

Sam was bold, 'Yes, maybe your grace, but what if she was here unofficially? You know, perhaps hidden by Shakespeare without Sir Alexander's knowledge. Is there no secret passage or priest-hole or anything here?'

'Not really. The only conceivable place would be the storage-rooms, now mostly full of junk, that lie beneath the kitchens'

'Are they past that no entry sign in the hallway there?'

'That's right. If you are not bothered by the risk of getting dirty you are welcome to look down there, but I won't join you if you don't mind'.

They thanked their hostess profusely and walked with her across the Inner Courtyard to the kitchens where Lady Rosanna gave authority for their access.

'Oh Sam I don't know. Can you imagine a queen agreeing to live in one of these tiny hovels?'

'Depends. I mean if you are an escaped prisoner, which basically she would have been, wouldn't you accept anywhere just to stay free?'

'That's true, plus her Shakespeare would be around'.

They reached a bend in the corridor off which rose another staircase. Sam went up it and tried the door but it was locked. 'Maybe that's an access to the outside without going through the kitchens. I don't know, I can't really get my bearings'

'Well I reckon we've done brilliantly Samuel. Shall we have a late lunch? I remember a lovely old pub in the village where we ate during the conference. We poor students weren't provided with the fodder laid on up here for the delegates'.

The pub was genuinely old, maybe four or five hundred years. Kate sat at a small table in the centre of the room, next to an impressive stout oak vertical support beam. Sam returned from the bar with drinks and menus to find an agitated Kate. Despite the absence of other customers she whispered to him, 'Sam you won't believe this. I was just gazing mindlessly at this post and look' She indicated a spot at about head level as they sat. 'I thought this was some modern angry graffiti, or even obscene advice, until I saw that the 'c' is actually an 'l'. Just here' Kate pointed to some tiny scratching on the timber.

Sam tried to read it 'Fulke Alice. What does that mean?'

'Fulke is a man's name isn't it? You know Fulke Walwyn the racehorse trainer. But what intrigues me Sam is that I'm sure I read somewhere that Shakespeare had a friend at Hoghton called something similar to that. His surname was Gwilliam or something'

'William and Gwilliam, you're winding me up yea?'

Kate laughed. 'You cynical bastard. No honestly. But who is Alice?'

'Well if they carved their names they must have been sweethearts'

Kate smiled at him as she pushed her face close to his, 'Sweethearts! Ooh what a lovely old-fashioned word. You're just a big soft old romantic aren't you'

'Hey less of the old you'

She put on a mock straight face 'Well one thing you have shown me Mr. Woodhouse is that whatever else, age is less important than size'

'Sshh! You young woman will get us barred from every hostelry in northern England. Now what are you having to eat?'

'I'm too excited, a bag of crisps will do'

As they entered Kate's cottage that evening she picked up a note which had been pushed through the letterbox. She read it out loud 'I called for you to go to the football. No answer so I assume you are either out or upstairs shagging your crumblie. And forget friendship O.K.'. Kate shrugged her shoulders nonchalantly, 'Stupid little boy!' she exclaimed as she threw the piece of paper in the wastebin.

Sam who was looking serious with pursed lips 'fraid I've ruined your relationship there Kate'

'Relationship? It wasn't a relationship Sam. Now come upstairs fella and I'll show you what a relationship is'. She turned provocatively 'or is it a liaison?'

Sam pushed past her as he called out 'Right but last one into the bedroom gets breakfast tomorrow'. Kate stuck her foot out and he tumbled to the carpet. She stood astride him chuckling, lifted her skirt and waggled herself then said 'Ok. - good idea sir' and strode calmly to the staircase, dropping her tee-shirt over her shoulder as she went.

Chapter Nineteen

A small young girl was waiting for Shakespeare as he left the classroom. 'Please sir I am to tell you that Sir Alexander wishes to see you immee.., imm.., right away'. She blushed and ran off.

Will's heart sank, *This can only be bad news* he decided. *I'll warrant I am to be told to send Marie away from here.*

His conclusions seemed to be confirmed by his employer's opening words 'Shakespeare I have today received some ill news'. Will braced himself to hear the worst. 'My physician tells me that he can not see me living beyond the month of August, so he is talking of only weeks'.

Selfish relief would best describe the emotion felt by the young teacher, but in fairness he did say 'Oh Sir Alexander I hope your doctor's diagnosis is erroneous'

'I fear not William. Now, the reason that I have summoned you here is twofold. Firstly I think you know in what high esteem I hold you and Fulke Gyllom. Although comparative newcomers to my household you have both displayed admirable enthusiasm and diligence in the conducting of your duties, as teachers and as players when required'

'Thank you sir'

'By way of gratitude I wish to personally acquaint you with two of the terms of my will'. Shakespeare looked puzzled. 'I have decreed that you and Gyllom, upon my death, will each receive the sum of forty shillings, but, and this is more important, let me see what is the exact wording?', he scrambled amongst the parchments on his desk. 'Ah yes here, "I most heartily require the said Sir Thomas...", my half-brother who is to inherit' he explained. 'Yes, "Sir Thomas to be friendly unto Fulk Gillam and William Shakeshaft..." your names whilst here of course, he reminded them. "...now dwelling with me and either to take them into his service or else to help them to some good master, as my trust is he will ".' He looked up at Shakespeare 'In fact William I have since spoken with Thomas and he will have no need of players or the costumes and musical instruments. I see your talents as being perhaps more inclined to the drama than the schoolroom and we have therefore agreed that you and Fulke will pass to my good friend Sir Thomas Hesketh at Rufford Hall, some ten miles west of here'.

Will remained silent. He had received a shock but one which was less traumatic than that which he had been expecting.

His employer spoke again 'One thing else William. Since I am not to be long for this world I have little to fear and my life can hardly be threatened by the Protestant raiders. Therefore, and if you are prepared to take the risk, I would be prepared to take into employment another teacher at Hoghton. I was considering perhaps a teacher of French'. Will could see a broad smile amidst the heavy growth of Sir Alexander's dark beard as he suggested 'I thought we might offer a post to that young boy who rescued you last Sunday, if he is still at hand'.

Shakespeare perhaps defied protocol as he grasped Sir Alexander's hand and firmly shook it.

The old man continued 'And Will tomorrow we must provide a bedroom for our Queen. God knows where she is at this moment or where she will sleep tonight'

'Thank you sir, thank you kindly'. Will bowed over-deferentially and withdrew walking backwards as though his employer too was a monarch.

He halted in his rearward progress as Lord Hoghton spoke again, in a mock-formal tone 'Shakespeare I feel that the new tutor should publicly arrive tomorrow morning, and that she should be a male. Comprenez-vous?'.

Will grinned as he reached the door.

Mary's sadness at the news of Sir Alexander's imminent death was multiplied when Will told her of his magnanimous gesture in acknowledging her presence officially; albeit if this did involve a change of gender. She would be losing another of her loyal supporters and each of these she considered as precious.

'But William is it not wonderful that we can now walk freely in the open together? Merveilleux!'

'Yes ma cherie but there can be no tumbles in the meadows whilst you are a boy. I don't want to be the subject of whispers'

Mary giggled, 'Well you could always wear a dress, that would confuse them and really set the tongues wagging. Oh Will how will I sleep in here tonight? I keep thinking there may be rats amongst these sacks of flour. Would you stay with me my love?'

'Oh Marie forgive me, I have not told you, what with all the other happenings. Fulke is staying in the village tonight, with his latest grand passion, you know, Alice. So he has offered you his bed in our room, then tomorrow Sir Alexander is arranging that a bedroom be fitted out for you'

'And you as well Will I trust?'

'Well I couldn't ask that of him, but I am sure he will be providing a sumptuous bed for you, and I suspect he knows where I will be laying my head'

'Here mon cheri, right here' and she clasped his face to her chest.

Will waited with Fulke until all of the others had left the dinner-table then they helped themselves to some of the remaining food; Shakespeare smuggling out a pheasant, some cheeses and bread rolls whilst Gyllom grabbed a jug of wine and three goblets.

In the dim light of dusk they followed the walls round to the kitchens and blindly descended the steps. Fulke was looking rather concerned as they approached Mary's door, 'Will I hope your lady will not berate me for my treatment of Angelique'

'Well Gyllom I cannot guarantee that she will not but I am sure that your granting of your bed to her, so unselfishly' he added sarcastically, 'will help to mollify her distress'.

Will knocked the door before entering. Mary ran and hugged him, causing bread rolls to scatter across the floor. 'Oh Will how thoughtful' she laughed, 'and pheasant too'. Fulke tried to pre-empt any admonishment by flourishing the jug of claret and brandishing the pewter goblets above his head.

'Umm, Mister Gyllom, the breaker of young maidens' hearts' she scolded, but could not maintain her severity as she offered her hand. 'It pleases me to see you again Fulke and I understand I must thank you for sacrificing your bed. I trust you will find another that is even more comfortable...or comforting'.

Both youths were stirred by that incredible smiling smirk. Gyllom then surprised even his best friend by announcing 'Tonight your majesty I will ask of Alice if she can give me one or two of her dresses, for a poor woman who has been taken in up at the Tower here'. The trio laughed together then Fulke added 'She has not your height and is a lot less slender, but if you wish I can ask her'

'Oh Gyllom you are truly a kind fellow. I am not surprised that you are chased by these young girls'

'Chased?' Will exaggerated the querying note in his voice, 'Perhaps a stag Marie but I think he is the hunter'

'No Will you do not do me fair. I am but a pawn in their games'. Fulke's expression of innocence fooled no-one.

'Tosh!' was Will's response.

Mary intervened 'Come lads let us not bicker, even in jest. I feel you are both as bad, for Will look how you forced your way into my castle'

'Marie!' then her expression reminded him what a tease she could be.

'Oh William I have such a hunger'. Luckily she did not see the hefty nudge that Fulke gave Will, then she picked up the pheasant and began to eat it from her fingers

'Oh Marie I forgot to bring a plate and cutlery'

'Worry not mon cher, it tastes even better like this' and she raised her glass and led the toast 'To freedom!'.

Fulke left for his trek down to Hoghton village and Will took Mary's hand and led her up to the courtyard and across to his room.

They threw the two mattresses onto the floor before slowly undressing each other and once more enjoying each other through the hours of darkness - a night which prompted one teacher to compliment her pupil on his learning ability and the other teacher to marvel at his tutor's capacity of knowledge.

In the dining-room the following morning Will and Mary, or Stewart, were the focus of attention. A number of the other staff and some of the bolder pupils approached them during the course of their breakfast, acts of intrusion which none of them would have attempted had they been aware of the true identity of the newcomer.

One lad, almost the same age as Will, was daring enough, and also impudent, to ask her 'Sir have you been given a job merely because you helped Mr. Shakespeare or can you really speak good French?'

Mary could not resist this opportunity to talk in the only language which she had been fluent in before she was sixteen years old. Her knowledge of English had been little better than her Greek and Latin. She gushed out a stream of sentences that left the doubter open-mouthed as he walked away. Mary smiled as she whispered to Will 'Can you imagine the Queen of France not being able to speak French?'

They were still chuckling when young Samuel Baker of the ever-ready tongue stood by them and spoke to Mary 'Please sir do you play football, because we all love it. We were given a ball by the qu...'

'Samuel!' Shakespeare interrupted curtly, for the boys had been sworn never to talk of their encounter with Mary Queen of Scots. 'Who was it gave you the ball Sam?'

The youngster showed admirable initiative as he answered 'Why sir it was the choirboy who left us last month, as I was saying sir'.

Mary patted Sam's arm 'I am afraid laddie that much as I love to watch football I am not an expert player. At times I feel I am a leg short'.

As Baker walked solemnly away Will muttered into Mary's ear 'Well at times I find I have a leg too many'.

She slapped his thigh under the table and could not suppress a loud and almost dirty laugh which turned heads. 'I know of that Mister Shakespeare for I have often made use of it myself, non?'. Those still staring at the couple wondered why Will's face had suddenly turned a deep red.

As they were leaving the room a boy was waiting for Will and he announced that Sir Alexander wished to speak with him and Master McQueen.

Hoghton bowed as they entered his room, 'Your Majesty may I formally welcome you to Hoghton Tower. I wish to apologise for the circumstances since your arrival'

'Lord Hoghton please, we both know that my being here is of such a nature that any other treatment would have been impossible. I would thank you however for your act of generosity at this time'.

Sir Alexander nodded an acknowledgement and explained 'Your Highness...'

'I think sir that it would be unwise to preserve such forms of address, particularly since they are temporarily inappropriate for a teacher called McQueen' she gently smiled. 'You may address me as Stewart for that is a noble name equal to any majesty or highness'.

'I take your point ma'am - sir. I believe Shakespeare will have told you that a room is being prepared for you, I regret I have no banner of the Fleur-de-Lys or Saint Andrew to drape there'.

Shakespeare knew he had spoken out of turn as soon as he opened his mouth 'Or indeed the Cross of Saint George sir'. Reproving smiles were directed at him as he lowered his head.

Sir Alexander looked gravely at him 'Indeed William, but in this current climate it would be unwise to proclaim such sentiments.

Now Stewart..., I am sorry your Majesty I find that most difficult to utter; what I wish to say is that I feel that your time may hang heavy upon you for I can only offer you some one or perhaps two hours of teaching and that only if you truly wish to actively teach'

'Yes sir indeed I do desire to teach. Apart from which a tutor without lessons would surely excite gossip'. She thought before continuing 'If I may make a request sir it is that I be provided with materials to indulge my passion for embroidery and sewing'

'Certainly...'sir'. I will speak with my wife Elisabeth and she will bring some to your room. Now if I may I will accompany you there myself. William do you wish to come with us?'

Mary answered for him 'I think it may be necessary for Will to know the whereabouts of my quarters Lord Hoghton'. Will's head returned to where it had been after his earlier violation of protocol, with chin on chest. Mary took his arm and whispered 'Come mon beau, I am sure Sir Alexander is a man of the world enough to have guessed at our, I believe you use the French word, liaison' and she directed a smile at his lordship whereby it was rendered impossible for the nobleman to disapprove of their situation.

The bedroom was large and well furnished. Sir Alexander explained that it was used by his half-brother Rowland whenever he made one of his extremely rare visits, '...and I do not anticipate him calling on me even if he were to know of my precarious state of health. I always thought the room to be very sombre, it was to Roland's taste, but my wife Elizabeth had her seamstresses working until late last night to make these new drapes for you ma'am, the room seems transformed. I hope you will be comfortable here your majesty'

Will was beginning to wish he had not accompanied them as she announced to his employer that 'I am sure *we* will be Lord Hoghton. Ooh look Will what a luxurious bed, better than my one at Bolton is it not?'

Sir Alexander showed no sign of having heard her last remark as he bowed politely and withdrew. Mary grabbed both of Shakespeare's hands and spun him round and round then slowed to a standstill, 'Ah my poor Will was embarrassed. Come fellow lets try this for size' and she ran across the room and flung herself onto the bed, spread-eagling her arms and her long legs, surprising him by her remarkable agility and unregal behaviour. In fact his dazzled expression provoked even more joy in this so happy Queen of Scots.

Chapter Twenty

'But Sam I know from my research that Shakespeare was only at Hoghton Tower from 1580 to '81, 1579 at the earliest'.

They were sitting in Kate's kitchen eating brunch, still in their dressing gowns.

'Which means...?' he led her

'Which means that if that was the time he was with Mary then it was before he married Anne Hathaway because that was November 1582, and she had been pregnant since the August'

'But you said it was a shotgun wedding and that they weren't in a continuing relationship'

'So?'

'Well couldn't he have...? Oh I don't know. Are you sure he left Hoghton in '81?'

'Yes because Sir Alexander Hoghton, his employer, died in August that year, the fifth I think, and his will apparently requests that his brother take care of Shakespeare and his colleague Fulk Gillam. It mentions a William Shakeshafte but it is now acknowledged that this was the Bard. Some academics reckon that the two youths actually passed into the service of a friend of Alexander's, Sir Thomas Hesketh'

'Hesketh!' Sam exclaimed, 'That was the name of my grandfather's landlord. Pa had a farm at Towcester, in Northamptonshire, and the Heskeths owned it. Their son, also called Alexander strangely enough, ran the Hesketh Formula One team in the seventies, you know - James Hunt'

'Really? Yes I bet that's the same family. In those days they lived at Rufford Old Hall, not far from Hoghton. Strange link though Sam'

'Destiny my dear. There was no way I could have escaped from meeting you my sexy Kismet - in fact Kismet Kate' and he burst out laughing.

In the afternoon they drove out to the Trough of Bowland and walked in the hills.

'Sam' said Kate as she shook the hand she was holding, 'There's one thing that bothers me a lot'. He raised his eyebrows in question. 'Ok if it is accepted that Shakespeare was a Catholic in his youth and if we, you and I, believe he had a love affair with Mary Queen of Scots, how come some of his plays contain anti-Rome sentiments?'

'Well he could have changed his religion but I think more likely is that it was a facade. It may have been just political expediency, you know, a need to conform in order to succeed in his career. I mean if the monarch, Elizabeth that is, is closely linked with the theatre then you're not going to get many plays performed if you're writing anti-Protestant propaganda are you?'

'I agree, but the plays don't all criticise Catholicism do they?'

'No, and even when they do they sometimes appear to reflect an involvement with that faith; like Old Hamlet's Ghost for instance who talks of being, what is it? 'doomed to the fires until the foul crimes done in my days of nature are burnt and purged away' - purged - purgatory - Catholic thing?'

'Right. And the Verona priest in Romeo and Juliet, he got a good write-up'

'True, but other times Shakepeare really slags off the Pope. In fact he seemed to be more anti-Pope than anti-Catholicism itself. I mean in King John, and I know this because I was looking at it again last week when you were in London, King John says "Tell him this tale; and from the mouth of England, and this much more, that no Italian priest shall tithe or toll in our dominions". That priest is the Pope who was trying to scrounge money off John. He finishes by saying "So tell the Pope, all revenues set apart, to him and his usurp'd authority".

'Umm I am impressed. I don't know King John at all. But Kate getting back to Mary, why if he was so in love with her, or had been by the time he wrote King John... when?'

'1591'

'Yes, so ten years after he met her why would he, apart from being pc., be so vociferous against the Pope?'

'Perhaps because the Pope did naff-all to help Mary in her predicament'

'Good point. I mean he wasn't writing anti-Mary at that time because she had been dead for four years by then. Anyway although Mary was a leading Roman Catholic she was even criticised by other Catholics for being excessively tolerant towards the Protestants. Did you know Kate that in her first year after landing back in Scotland she arranged for one sixth of all church benefices to be given to the poverty-struck Protestant ministers? In fact it was said, after her death of course, like all unjustly killed martyrs, that she was a victim of being ahead of her time in religious tolerance. She really did believe in mercy and justice for all so it's all a bit sick that she should end up with such a tragic fate'

'God you do feel strongly Sam and I can see why'

'Too right, and I'm not even a catholic. Shit she even read Latin with George Buchanan, the Protestant leader, and he ended up dedicating his translation of the Psalms to Mary'. Sam suddenly stopped in his tracks 'Hey Kate, getting back to Shakespeare's plays I've just remembered something'. Now it was her turn to look wide-eyed. 'When I was at university I did a unit on Shakespeare myself and I wrote one of my essays on *The Tempest*'

'Yes?'

'Yes. I used to invent arguments just for fun sometimes. I had this incredibly brilliant lecturer for seminars and he seemed to appreciate my ideas. Richard Wilson, you could ask him a question and you'd never get a direct answer but he'd give you five or six other snippets of useful information instead. Now this was obviously before I ever met you so I had never heard of Shakespeare being considered as a Roman Catholic. I suggested that in the name Prospero, who as you know ruled his own island world, controlling the waves and nature etcetera, that from his name you could extract, and in sequence, P-O-P-E. I claimed that Shakespeare was depicting Prospero as a sort of God-like figure and was thereby reflecting another who was viewed by Rome in the same way'

'That's cool. You see Sam you were leading yourself towards all this'

'Yes but I didn't know the journey would take me to a twenty-three year-old nymphomaniac'

'Right that's it! I've been waiting for a chance to take a rest' and Kate grabbed Sam and wrestled him to the ground. 'There's no-one about Mister Woodhouse and I have my reputation to live down to' she chuckled as she slipped off her white mini.

They were still soaking the sun into their bare bodies, lying on the flattened grass, when Kate spoke 'Sam I wonder when and why they split. I assume they did finish before her death, I mean he got married and had Susanna in May of '83 so presumably he wasn't carrying on an affair with Mary then'

'Meanwhile back in academia...' Sam muttered as he continued lazily stroking Kate's flat stomach.

They picked up some take-away Chinese on the way home. As they finished eating Kate suggested 'Let's forget the brain-bashing for this evening and watch some telly shall we?'.

They snuggled close on the sofa but after half an hour of some mediocre film Sam suggested 'Lets forget the telly for this evening and go to bed shall we?'.

'I thought you'd never ask' and Kate tickled his ribs and sprinted upstairs, calling out 'Right that's you get breakfast again tomorrow, haaaah!'

For Kate and Sam the rest of that week was a perfect idyll, a fulfilling mixture of studying and making love.

Chapter Twenty-One

For Will and Mary the rest of that week was a perfect idyll, a fulfilling mixture of teaching and making love.

On the Sunday morning Mary was delighted to discover that a Holy Mass was to be held in the Oak Parlour. All members of the household were required to attend; even Fulke dragged himself away from the charms of Alice and made the early-morning hike up the driveway from the village. Mary of course had to attend as Stewart.

The tranquillity of the incense-laden room was suddenly shattered as the door burst open and there stood five severe-looking men with drawn swords. Mary's hand gripped Will's tightly. Brackenby walked to the front of the congregation and confronted the now increasingly frail Sir Alexander, sitting swathed in a blanket despite the warmth of midsummer. 'Lord Hoghton I arrest you in the name of Queen Elizabeth on the charge of conducting an illegal ceremony, namely the seditious practice of a papist Mass'.

'To whom am I speaking you ignorant fellow, and how dare you invade a place of worship in this manner?' It was difficult for Alexander to sound aggressive with his weak voice.

Without answering Brackenby turned to one of his colleagues 'Digby count the heads here'. He again addressed his lordship, at the same time running his eyes over the gathered throng, 'You are further under suspicion of harbouring an escaped prisoner. I speak of Mary Stuart known as the Queen of the Scots. I have here a list of the persons resident in your house. Each one will walk to the front upon hearing their name called. They will then be taken outside and searched'

'And what pray sir do you think they may be concealing at such a holy gathering?'

'Their identity!' snapped the intruder.

Will and Mary were positioned by the wood-panelled wall and he now began to slowly lead her along it towards the side-door to the adjoining room which then passed out into the Inner Courtyard. They had just opened the door a crack, hoping to be concealed by the heads of their companions, when a voice rang out 'Halt you two there!'. The pair now abandoned all subtlety and dashed into the next room and turned immediately left, throwing the door open and sprinting across the yard past the Upper Gatehouse and into the kitchen-building. As they ran they heard the clatter of boots chasing them. Will turned to wait but Mary had kept up with him and together they pattered down the stone steps and ran along the subterranean corridor. Outside Mary's previous room Will spoke for the first time 'Marie, up here' and he leaped up another staircase and flung open the heavy door. Two crossed swords barred their way.

The Lower Courtyard was filling as the congregation arrived to see a bullying man confronting Will Shakeshafte and Stewart McQueen. They could not hear everything that was being said.

His voice was pompous as he proclaimed 'Mary Queen of Scots, on the orders of her most royal majesty Queen Elizabeth you are to be taken back to Bolton Castle and then you, together with such of your entourage as is seen fit, will be moved to Tutbury Castle in Staffordshire'. Brackenby dropped his formal tone as he sneeringly told her 'which you will find to be very different from your previous so-called prison'. All form of correct address to a monarch had now been forgotten by the smirking captor. He turned to Will, still holding his lover's hand. 'And you sir are in trouble. Not only have you aided in the escape of a prisoner, the most important prisoner in the land to our Majesty, but you are also charged with the poaching of deer from the estates of Sir Thomas Lucy at Charlecote in the county of Warwickshire'.

Mary was almost shouting as she interrupted 'No Brackenby! You are mistaken. Will played no part in my escape. Yes I fell in love with him when he came to Bolton Castle but it was purely my idea to seek to join him here at Hoghton. Neither he nor Sir Alexander knew of my scheme until I arrived dressed as I am now. Lord Hoghton, until you arrived, believed me to be a male youth and has engaged me as a tutor of French'. She made the sign of the cross over her chest.

'A youth madam, and male? I think not' and Brackenby tore off Mary's cap to release her russet mane, provoking a mass gasp from the congregation which was witnessing a scene beyond their belief. As they recognised Queen Mary they dropped to their knees as one, genuflecting as they did so. 'On your feet you vassals' bawled Brackenby. Nobody moved. He turned to Mary 'Your claim will be further inquired into and if found lacking then you Mister Shakespeare will be collected from Hoghton and taken to the Tower'.

Will flinched and Mary screamed a hysterical 'No!'.

Mary was permitted, accompanied by two armed guards, to return briefly to her room with Will. Her authoritarial tone, at it's grandest, left no doubt in the men's minds that they would remain outside the closed door while she and Will bade their goodbyes, or hopefully au revoirs.

As Will shut the door she walked across to pick up her little embroidered silk purse, the only possession that she had brought on her flight from Bolton Castle, stuffed inside her doublet. She turned to Will 'Mon cheri this diamond ring was sent to me by the Queen of England, my *dear* cousin Elizabeth' she added with a sarcastic edge to her adjective. 'It is one of a pair for I don't know if you are aware of it Will but apparently it is an English custom to give such a ring as a sign of amity and if one of the couple is in distress then she or he returns the ring, to recall friendship and to seek help. Rather hypocritical in her case was it not? I feel it would serve little use were I to send it to London eh Will? She has a similar ring and when the two are laid together the diamonds form the shape of a heart'. Mary kissed him gently. 'My darling I give you this ring. It may prove useful if ever you do cross Elizabeth and hopefully she would respect, even after my death, how strongly I have felt for you'.

Tears were now flooding down Will's cheeks, 'Marie this is not the end of us. It cannot be'

Mary wrapped her arms tightly around him and lay her head on his shoulder 'Of course it is not my dearest. Be stout lad, you have a woman who loves you more than any I have before. We will meet again, I promise you'.

'I swear that to you too you my darling' and now he uncontrolledly sobbed, his whole body heaving.

'Come Will, we have already shared some weeks together that most people never have in a lifetime. There will be more my brave lover'.

An insistent thudding on the door interrupted their passionate kiss of farewell.

Fulke had his arm clasped round Shakespeare as they stood watching Mary climb up onto her magnificent stallion before having her wrists bound and lead-ropes being run from the horse's bridle to each of two of her guards. It was as well for her captors that she was such an expert horsewoman for only a competent rider could remain in the saddle thus encumbered. She could not even wave to Will but turned her fragile face towards him as the little cortege began its long and necessarily slow ride back to Bolton Castle. Will blew her a kiss and raised his arm limply to wave before turning away distraught and being consoled by the faithful Fulke.

Eventually his eyes returned to the distant group of riders in time to watch them disappear, taking away the woman who would prove to be the greatest love of his life.

Chapter Twenty-Two

On the breakfast tray Sam had brought up an envelope addressed to Kate on which he had seen the franking of Lancaster University. As she saw it her smile evaporated, 'Oh Christ I bet I know what this is'. Sam climbed in beside her as she opened it. 'Shit shit shit!'

Sam looked worried 'Kate?'

'Oh Sam I hate Monday post, its always bills or bad news or something crap'

'Bad news?'

She handed him the sheet of paper, explaining 'I'd forgotten all about this. Its months since I applied'.

Sam read the short letter: 'Dear Miss Courtney, We are pleased to inform you that your application for the temporary placement with the Universita di Verona has been approved. Please contact the Postgraduate Secretary in the English Department for further details as soon as possible. This is a matter of some urgency since your departure date will be 5 August'.

'August the fifth, that's Thursday' frowned Sam

'I know. Oh Sam!'. Her man wrapped his arm round her as she miserably continued 'I had this idea, for a break as much as anything, to visit the cities of North East Italy, those connected with Shakespeare's plays: Padua, Verona, Venice, Mantua you know'

'Well, it could be interesting Kate', but his forced attempt to console her fell on deaf ears.

'Bollocks Sam! Just as, for the first time in my life I feel content, no not content, totally happy, I have it ruined by this'

'Do you have to go?'

'That's the point, if I don't then there will be repercussions. I'd probably lose future funding to complete my doctorate because it would be seen as a lack of commitment'

'How long is it for Kate?'

'Six fucking months' she answered angrily, but her venom was not directed at him. 'Sam can you come with me?'

'Oh Kate I'd love to lass but its just impossible at the moment. I'm totally strapped for cash'

Kate started to sob, the first time really that Sam had seen her anything but happy.

'Come on lets lie close' he said and lay down, pulling the duvet over them. 'We'll sort something out. I don't want to lose you for one day never mind six months'.

That afternoon Sam went with Kate onto her university campus. Before going to the secretary's office they went for a meeting with her tutor where, with Sam's assistance, Kate divulged their theory about Shakespeare and the catholic Queen of Scots and hence the change of direction of her thesis. 'So you see Tony, Italy isn't all that relevant now'

'Kate what do you mean? It's the centre of Roman Catholicism'

'Yes but not Scottish' she answered rather petulantly.

'Kate you'll to have to go there. You know how the financial machinery works in these places'. He turned to Sam as they all stood up 'And good luck with your book Sam, with this girl's brains working with you I'm expecting two masterpieces'.

Both of them smiled weakly and shook his hand.

Sam drove Kate to Manchester Airport to catch her flight to Verona. At passport control she flung her arms round him, gripping him tightly, her eyes already moist. 'Sam I love you so much. Promise me we'll speak every night'. Sam nodded, too choked to speak.

She passed by the blank-faced official then turned to wave, tears flooding down her cheeks. Sam raised a limp arm and blew her a kiss with his other hand before she disappeared into the throng of happy tourists.

Chapter Twenty-Three

The tragic day of Shakespeare, when he lost his beloved Marie, became a devastating week when, only three days later, with Mary re-confined back at Bolton Castle, Sir Alexander Hoghton died. Many considered that the violent invasion of his home had been the final straw, precipitating a complete loss of the will to live.

There followed three days of mourning when nothing took place at Hoghton Tower. Lessons were suspended and time weighed heavily on the distraught Will and his friend Fulke, although they did spend a lot of time down at the Red Lion. Gyllom, with his Alice, tried to console the ruined Shakespeare who was drinking himself into a stupor.

'In God's name Fulke in three days I have lost two of the most important people in my life. Is it any wonder that I have lost my reason? I am without my lover and my father-figure'

'Will, you know how you sometimes write a poem when you are upset, can you not...?'

'Fulke how could I put all of these feelings into a mere poem? No, one day I will write a play about such a situation'.

Sunday was normally a free day for the staff, apart from attending the 'illicit service' if they wished, but this week Will and Fulke had to load their belongings onto one of the carts and be taken to Rufford to join their new master Sir Thomas Hesketh.

Fulke asked the driver to halt at the inn where Alice was waiting outside, her face already reddened and wet when they arrived.

'Alice my darling do not take on so. I am to be but ten miles away, it is not the other side of the world'

'Ten miles or ten thousand...' choked the girl 'how will I ever see you Fulke?'

He paused then, quick-thinking as ever, came up with an idea, 'Alice my little jewel, I will get Shakespeare here to teach me to ride and will somehow persuade Sir Thomas, or maybe just his groom, to lend me a horse each Sunday. Thereby will I come to you. We will have the afternoons together'

Alice's chubby face broke into a sad smile. 'Promise me Fulke. He will won't he Will?'

'I'll bully him if he doesn't lass. But I know Fulke, he won't want to stay away from your arms'

'Or the rest of you my little minx'. This time Fulke raised a chuckle from his girl, but her tears poured again as they headed west.

It became immediately obvious that Shakespeare and Gyllom were virtually surplus to requirements at Old Hall for they were given only a few hours teaching and their thespian talents would have been better appreciated had they been musical abilities. Sir Thomas's Players, of whom Sir Alexander has spoken to Will, proved to be principally musicians who performed only the occasional play in the Great Hall.

Fulke did grasp the basics of horsemanship and kept his promise to Alice. She was ecstatic because the paucity of lessons meant that Fulke was able to return to Rufford on Monday mornings, although his hush-payments to the groom were eroding into his forty shillings inheritance.

Some eight weeks into their engagement by Lord Hesketh yet another upheaval occurred in the lives of Will and Fulke. Rufford Old Hall was visited by The Earl of Derby's Men, the company of touring players of the fourth Earl, Henry Stanley, a man who was an active supporter of the cause of Mary Queen of Scots and who had found himself in trouble as a result on more than one occasion. Derby and Hesketh were friends, in fact Lord Hesketh's son Robert had married Mary Stanley, the daughter of a cousin of the Earl, and furthermore Sir Alexander Hoghton's wife Elizabeth was related to Sir Thomas Hesketh. By the time of this visit by the players Will and Fulke had been complaining to their employer about the lack of opportunity to express their dramatic abilities. Following a discussion that evening between the two noblemen they summoned the two young actor-teachers and offered them the chance to join the Earl of Derby's band of players. This was the only ray of brightness in the gloomy life of Will, an existence which was growing ever darker as he missed his beloved queen more and more.

Chapter Twenty-Four

Kate was strolling miserably in the early-afternoon drizzle, head down. She turned onto the deserted wide promenade of the Piazza Bra in Verona. The impressive Roman amphitheatre, L'Arena, was across the square to her right and on her left was the string of clone-like green-canopied bars and restaurants. Halfway along she heard, for probably the hundredth time in the past two weeks, *'Ciao bella!'*. She ignored the cliché, used by a host of Italian males and a line which she already considered to be pathetic. She increased her step to accelerate away when the voice rang out again 'Hey *piano piano* chuck'. Kate stopped and spun round disbelieving. There half-way back amidst the rows of empty tables in the gloom of the tenting was her fella.

'Sam!' she screamed and hurtled towards him, barging into a table on the front row and spilling their cappucinos over the three Germans sitting there. She leaped up at him, wrapped her legs around his hips and kissed him hard. 'Oh you wonderful bastard you didn't tell me you were coming, not even last night'

'Well...' Sam was choked again but this time the tears were of joy.

Kate slid her legs down to the ground. 'But how come? How did you get here? You had no money'.

'I walked'.

'You silly sod!'

'Kate its all a bit fantastic really. Mike, you know my agent, has negotiated me a five-thousand pound advance on my book on Mary and Will. And as I told you on the phone I'm making it a novel rather than a history text. Apparently the publisher thinks it could be a big one, maybe a film too'

'Shit Sam that's incredible. Come on my man lets get out of this weather, my hotel is only just round the corner' and she linked her arm through his as they walked out into the happy rain.

The next day Kate became a tourist guide as she took Sam around the 'Shakespeare spots' of Verona. First stop was number 23 via Capello, just off the Piazza Erbe. The thirteenth century house, better known as the home of the Bard's Juliet Capulet, is entered through an archway now inscribed with literally thousands of graffitied names, each one densely overlaying the others.

'Fancy looking for a W and an M?' Kate joked. 'And don't get all gooey about that balcony Sam' she said as they stood looking up at it from the small courtyard 'It was put there in the nineteenth century'.

They walked to the far end to examine the beautiful life-size bronze statue of Juliet. '1972' Kate informed him.

'But why is her right breast so shiny?'

'Because...Ah now you'll see' and they turned to see a crocodile of Japanese line up and take turns to step forward and place a hand on the statue whilst having their photo taken by thirty companions. 'For luck?' Sam asked. Kate nodded. 'Funny that because I always go for your left one first don't I?'

'So that's why its grown bigger' she laughed. 'Come on you're a tourist, you can't get horny yet'

'But I haven't rubbed her tit'

'She'd only seem inferior' Kate boasted with a huge grin as she dragged him into the house which they found to be an almost empty museum.

As they threaded their way out through the incoming nationalities Sam asked 'And is there a Romeo's house?'

Kate smiled then spoke in a superior tone 'Samuel do I need to remind you that the Montagues and the Capulets were actually fiction, but I grant you it is thought they were based on two real families. I'll show you the place which is claimed to be his home'.

It was only a couple of streets away. Sam read the plaque on the wall, which implied a certain un-italian sense of irony, for the lines read:

"O where is Romeo?

Tut I have lost myself; I am not here;
This is not Romeo, he's some other where"
Atto 1. Scena 1

'Umm' was Sam's dubious response. 'Maybe there *is* an italian with a subtle sense of humour'.

Kate tugged his arm 'Juliet's grave? - just to complete the set? We'll have to take a bus though, its quite a way'

'I'll walk if you will. I just want you to myself, not crammed in with a load of grockles'. Kate looked puzzled, 'Tourists' he explained. 'Tell you what though Kate, he certainly knew a bit about love did William'

'Must have had a good teacher. Bit like me I suppose' she grinned.

'You what! If anything I'm the pupil in this relationship. I thought I was experienced before I met you you vixen'.

Kate was not smiling, 'Seriously Sam I've only had two boyfriends before you and never sex like we have. I think we bring it out of each other'.

Sam took her hand and they were halfway across the wide road when they stopped to kiss, provoking the honking of forty Veronese horns as some cars passed to the left of them, some to the right, each of them cheering the couple out of their windows, while others just queued up in the middle of the road and watched this pair in the city of the famous lovers.

As they both sat eating spaghetti al vongole that evening Kate told Sam that they would have to make the short train journey to Padua on the Sunday evening because she had to attend the university there on Monday morning. 'You can have a look round Padua on Monday Sam, its a lovely city. My favourite place is the little Scrovegni chapel – it's in a garden off the main road from the train station into town. The whole curved ceiling is a navy-blue starlit sky and on the four walls are three rows of frescoes by Giotto which depict the story of the Bible'

'Sounds good, I prefer frescoes to paintings anyway and this is the country to see them'

'Then in the evening, you remember I told you about John, the guy who 'chatted up' Lady de Hoghton?' Sam smiled. 'Well he now lives in Piedmonte over in the northwest of Italy but I phoned him, because we swapped numbers at the conference, and he is coming over to Padua for a few days on Monday. He has a friend who lives there who he's known for about fourteen years I think he said. Her name is Elisabetta and we are all going out to dinner that night, is that O.K.?'

'Sounds brilliant. I've always loved Italian food and it will be nice to eat with a local'

Kate looked at her wrist 'Shit Sam we'll have to hurry up and finish and go home, its past our bedtime'. His watch read nine o'clock.

Elisabetta was stunning. Sam had imagined that she would be a female of about the same age as John, and indeed himself, but he estimated that she was only in her late twenties. Although she lived with her parents in Padua their background was the south and this was evident in her darker Mediterranean skin and flashing brown eyes. She and the plump middle-aged John formed an incongruous couple but it was obvious that theirs was a deep friendship.

Sam spoke 'Kate tells me you two have been friends for years John'

'Yes we've written to each other ever since we met when we were staying at the same holiday hotel in Lido de Jesolo. After that I visited her for a few days every year that I came to Italy on holiday. Eli was only a kid then'. He turned to her 'Quanti anni hai avuto quando noi abbiamo incontratti Eli?'

She smiled and put her hand on John's 'Solo quattordici, non ricordi?'

John translated 'Yes she was only fourteen when we first met. I remember we used to play football on the beach that summer. She had a terrific kick on her'. He turned and smiled at her.

'Foootball, calcio?' Elisabetta asked

'Si'

'Ma addesso hai sbagliato'

'No non e vero! She's telling me that now I've made a mistake because I support Inter Milan and she's a Juventina'. Eli laughed realising what John had told them and amused because she was unused to hearing him speak English.

Kate spoke 'Talking of football leads me to Preston to Hoghton Tower to Shakespeare'

'Subtle change of subject there Kate' grinned John,

'Yes Shakespeare. When you told me about your line of research I dug out a paper from the conference. Did you go to Anthony Gilbert's lecture?'

'No it clashed I think with one on power in King Lear'

'It was good -on Othello. Basically Tony's argument was that Othello and Iago are the two poles of Catholicism and Puritanism and that Othello is depicted as being infected, if you like, with superstitions and that this is a covert reference to the Catholic doctrine which of course couldn't be shown on the stage. Tony claims that during the play the prejudices against Catholicism, which most of Shakespeare's contemporary audience would have held, are shown to be unjustified'.

'In what way John?'

'Well, hang on I've written something down that Anthony said. Here we are: "Desdemona is condemned for her typical Papist practice" ie. sexual laxity which could be absolved in the confessional' John qualified. 'Like Iago's line that "In Venice they do let God see the pranks they dare not show their husbands. Their best conscience is not to leav't undone, but kept unknown". Then Tony goes on: "But Othello is wrong and merely represents a common prejudice against papists". And this was the punchline I reckon, "The effect of this recollection by Othello is to expose the damage prejudice does to innocent catholics ". Pretty strong stuff eh you guys? He's suggesting that the audiences maybe realised they shouldn't be so anti-catholic and might even be mistaken in their Reformation religion'

'Wow!' sighed Kate. 'Oh John, poor Eli is out of this'

'Yes I was about to tell her what we're talking about. Parliamo della commedia di Shakespeare. Otello, la sai?'

'Si certo, l'ho studiato alla scuola'.

Sam was puzzled, 'John I heard you say commedia, but Othello is a tragedy'

'Yes that used to confuse me. In Italian 'commedia' means a play, of any sort'.

The sweets arrived, gorgeous concoctions of fruit, ice-cream and liqueurs.

They left the restaurant and John got into Elisabetta's little Fiat Panda. Sam and Kate refused the offer of a lift and walked home in the warm Italian night.

'Nice guy' mused Sam

'Nice girl too, I thought your tongue was dropping out when we met her'

'No way. Sure she was nice to look at, in a latin way, but I always think that Italian girls are like beautiful butterflies and that when they grow older they turn back into caterpillars'

'You mean they like to crawl all over you' teased Kate

'Shut up woman. Give me a Lancashire lass who will last any time'

'That's if you don't burn me out you randy devil' and she pinched Sam's bottom and ran off, turning to call back over her shoulder 'Come on I want to see if your practice is as good as your preaching, mio amore! '.

Chapter Twenty-Five

That first week apart was for Mary even worse than was Will's. Upon her return to Castle Bolton she too was subjected to an enforced relocation, but her journey was a lot longer and fraught with problems. Queen Elizabeth had given the official reason for the move as being to provide Mary with a location 'more honourable and agreeable' for her but the truth was that it was thought necessary to remove the Scottish Queen from Lancashire, which was still a hotbed of recusant Catholicism, and which was also too near to Scotland for the English Queen's liking.

The journey itself was terrible. Mary Livingstone became ill and could not complete the trip, then plans were changed as it was realised that Tutbury Castle was not yet ready to receive her so her new jailer, the Earl of Shrewsbury, instructed that they should first go to another of his residences, Sheffield House. Upon arrival it was discovered that all the furniture had been transferred to Tutbury and so the entourage had to continue to its original destination. Mary's health also deteriorated on the journey for she was subject to digestive disorders and it was thought that she had a gastric ulcer, obviously exacerbated by the stress of her recapture and the subsequent nightmare journey.

At Tutbury Mary's morale was at a low ebb following the ecstatic heights of her time with young Shakespeare. She now found herself in a desolate place and her apartments in the fortress were damp and draughty, for the castle had not been properly maintained for many years - hardly the 'agreeable' conditions which Elizabeth had promised. The only positive note for Mary was that her keeper, George Talbot Earl of Shrewsbury, was known to be sympathetic to her cause, indeed Elizabeth had chosen him precisely for this reason, to allay suspicions should Mary be murdered whilst in his care. However, any satisfaction at having a considerate captor was to an extent negated by the antipathy of his new wife, the thrice-widowed Bess of Hardwicke. Worst of all for Mary of course was her separation from Will who was now some one hundred and twenty miles distant, and she saw no likelihood of contact with him.

Then, five weeks after her arrival the Earl, whom she had charmed, without deliberate intention, merely by her proximity to him, as she did all men who ever had contact with her, announced that he would allow her to send and receive correspondence. She would also be permitted to receive occasional visitors provided that he was given prior notice of their arrival.

When he came to personally announce this relaxation in restrictions Shrewsbury handed her two letters which he had been holding back from her. He had sensitively ignored Elizabeth's instruction that any mail be opened and censored.

As soon as she was alone Mary inspected the letters, the first one she recognised as being in the hand of Mary Livingstone who had made a recovery and hoped to join her mistress at the end of the month. The writing on the outside of the second was unknown to her as she opened it. She read only the opening address "My Darling Marie" before dropping to her knees and crossing herself before praying, with tears streaming down her pale porcelain face.

She gathered herself together and began to read the manuscript from her lover:

"Precious lady I fear there is little point in wishing that all is well with you. I know not Tutbury but whatever the conditions, be they sparse or sumptuous, I feel that you will be devastated as am I by our tragic separation. My Lord Alexander passed away immediately after your departure and I am now in the employ of Sir Thomas Hesketh at Old Hall, Rufford. What of my life here? Fulke and I are like, if you will pardon the expression my love, a pair of spare pizzles, for we teach rarely and have not yet trod a stage". Mary laughed aloud at this and felt secure that Will's 'pizzle' was in fact out of use. "We have made known our dissatisfaction to the Lord Hesketh but have succeeded in changing nothing. Marie I have scribbled some lines to try to convey the thoughts which surely you already know I feel, but I hope that seeing them written down will reinforce them for you:

How like a winter hath my absence been
From thee, the pleasure of the fleeting year!
What freezings have I felt, what dark days seen
What old December's bareness every where!
And yet this time removed was summer's time,
The teeming autumn, big with rich increase,
Bearing the wanton burden of the prime,
Like widow'd wombs after their lords' decease
Yet this abundant issue seem'd to me
But hope of orphans and unfather'd fruit;

For summer and his pleasures wait on thee,
And, thou away, the very birds are mute;
Or, if they sing, 'tis with so dull a cheer
That leaves look pale, dreading the winter's near.

I fear my dearest loved one that you will never see this letter, but should you do so I pray that a reply will be allowed you. I sense myself already closer at this thought and promise you, you who are my life, that we will again be together by some means.

Ever yours my wondrous Queen of the Heart.

William."

Mary Seton could not believe what she saw when she came to yet again attempt to console her mistress, for Mary was slowly dancing around the room holding aloft some sheets of parchment which she had just read for the twelfth time. The queen ran to hug her friend.

'Ma'am what brings this lightness to your soul?' Mistress Seton gasped as Mary spun her round.

''Will!' Mary screamed, 'My Will!'

Now the faithful lady herself was crying, 'Oh Marie how wonderful' she choked.

'Mary I am to be permitted to send letters, Shrewsbury has told me that this morn. I must reply to my man. He is now moved to Lord Hesketh at Rufford, yet still further from me I fear, but now closer in spirit' and this time her dance was faster.

Shakespeare's world was growing ever darker. He had sent a letter, including an attempt at a sonnet, to his lover some four weeks ago but had not as yet received a reply. His worst worry, that Mary would be barred from receiving mail, seemed to be confirmed.

Now he was to change employer again, joining the Earl of Derby's Players. The saving grace was that he and Fulke would definitely be expected to act in the plays being toured around the homes of the aristocracy in the North of England and the Midlands.

Will had been in the employ of the Earl of Derby for two weeks when a messenger from Lord Hesketh brought, amongst papers for the Earl, a letter addressed to William Shakespeare. There was but one person in the world that he would wish to hear from and that was deemed impossible so it was with an air of nonchalance that Will opened the document. He became delerious upon reading the opening greeting: "Mon cheri precieux Will ".

Whilst walking to his room to read in privacy Shakespeare was trembling. He sat down and read "Words cannot tell of what your letter did for my spirits. My darling I was resigned to end my life rotting away in worsening health in this miserable hole called Tutbury. The Earl of Shrewsbury has condescended to allow me correspondence, and your letter I received but this morning. I regret that you too Will have a less than ideal situation, but what is ideal? Perfection can only be when we are rejoined ". There followed a series of heartfelt sentiments, closing with a couplet:

"Time than fortune should be held more precious
For fortune is as false as she is specious ".

She had signed herself "Ta cherie Marie ".

An adjoiner had been added, dated two days later: "Will, the Earl has accepted that the grossly unsanitary and spartan conditions here at Tutbury are unbearable for me and he is to move me to another of his homes, one which I understand came with his marriage to the

Hardwicke woman, namely Chatsworth House, which I believe to be in Derbyshire.

M".

There followed yet another addition - "Will I would send you my heart but it is already with you. Guard it well my darling.

Marie".

Chapter Twenty-Six

Sam and Kate were sitting in the still warm evening at a table under the splendid clock tower which overlooks the Piazza dei Signore in the centre of Padua. To their left was the impressive Palace of Justice dividing this square from the Piazza delle Erbe where Kate had stocked up with fruit and vegetables.

Sipping their crodino aperitifs Kate turned to Sam 'Well fella we've done the tourist thing but haven't really talked about what you've been finding out'. But before he could speak she planted her glass down firmly 'Oh shit Sam this is hopeless, I should be back in England with you where I can research our idea. Sure Padua has a good uni but what's the point if the books are nearly all in Italian, and they know naff all about Mary Queen of Scots. I just feel I'm wasting my time here'. She put her hand on Sam's and mellowed 'Sorry love, we'll talk about that another time. C'mon man what have *you* got?'

Sam began rather self-consciously, not used to pronouncing his findings on demand, 'Well its strange and exciting in a way Kate because although I'm concentrating on the Mary half I find I'm always looking for how her life could have affected Shakespeare's way of thinking and perhaps even vice versa'

'Sam that's great. I reckon this is the only way we can do it, look at it as a sort of osmosis between them'

'Osmosis, yes, I haven't heard that word since fifth-form biology lessons, but you're spot on'

'Why thank you kind sir' and Kate leaned across the table and kissed him.

'No I wasn't being patronising Kate'

'I know that. I just felt like a quick snog. Carry on'

'Anyway as I was saying I think that we can assume that all of Mary's incredible life before she met Will would have been discussed between them. Now the big thing is, ok. she was Queen of France at one time and Queen of Scotland but the main niggle must have been how she had been conned out of the English throne'

'Did she really have a strong case then?'

'Certainly. As usual everything comes back to Henry the Eighth, I mean the whole Catholic versus Protestant argument stems from him as you know. What affected Mary particularly Kate was that he altered the Right of Succession, but it only lasted for the Tudor era'

'What do they call that Sam, what we have now, primogeniture isn't it when the crown passes down through the eldest son and so on?'

'Exactly. Oh Kate am I getting too heavy?'

'No darling please tell me because at the moment I can't see where you're heading'

'Ok, now Henry's three kids, the young Edward the sixth, Mary Tudor and Elizabeth all ruled, in that order'. Kate nodded. 'But Henry, through introducing the Act of Wills in 1540, was able to treat the monarchy as a piece of property in that instead of it passing down to the next-in-line by sex and age, i.e. by primogeniture, he could stipulate who would be the inheritors.'

'So where is Mary Stuart in all this?'

Sam drew a breath. 'She was the grand-daughter of Henry the Eighth's older sister Margaret Tudor who married James the Fourth of Scotland. Look Kate forgive me if I'm teaching you to suck eggs, you probably know this already'

'Sweet Sam I do love you. Carry on man'

'Right, Henry's younger sister was another Mary, she was married to Louis X11 of France and then to the Duke of Suffolk. Now because Henry's kids, the three direct descendants, died childless that would normally have led to his elder sister Margaret Tudor's offspring inheriting. Her son was James the Fifth of Scotland but he had died when his daughter Mary, our Mary, was only five days old and therefore the English monarchy should have passed on to her, Mary Queen of Scots. But, and this is where it all went wrong, the Suffolk branch of the family, from Henry's younger sister Mary, was Protestant and old man Henry had decreed in his will that the crown should go to them should his own children not produce an heir. That would have led to Lady Jane Grey becoming Queen except Mary Tudor had had her topped in 1554'

'But Sam, after Elizabeth died the crown went to James the First, the Sixth of Scotland, the son of Mary Queen of Scots'

'Bum bum! Which ironically reinforces the fact that Mary Queen of Scots should have been the rightful Queen of England if Elizabeth died before her, or even sooner according to the Catholic church, because they insisted that Elizabeth was a bastard because her mother Anne Boleyn was bigamously married to Henry and as you'll remember they didn't recognise his divorce from Catharine of Aragon'

'So Elizabeth shut Mary Stuart away then terminated her'

'End of story'

'Brilliant I've got all that sorted, now please I really want to know how you think this might have influenced Willie's work, but shall we pick up some pizzas and take them home first?'

'Good idea. Funny how you use the word willie in the same sentence as home though'

'Quite unconsciously' she grinned.

'Yea yea'

It was two o'clock in the morning when Kate rolled off Sam and sat up against her pillows.

'So?'

'So what madam?'

'So what about Will and Mary?'

'Oh them'

'Yes them. I mean they are the second most important thing in my life'

'And the first?' Sam fished

'That's obvious, Preston North End' and she tickled his ribs.

'Behave! This is it, the Woodhouse bombshell'. Kate was finally attentive, slipping her arm through Sam's as he spoke. 'I was talking about Mary being denied her inheritance by Henry the Eighth moving the goalposts right?'. Kate nodded and this time she was listening eagerly. 'Can you think of one of Master Shakespeare's plays where this happened too?' her man asked.

'Hang on'

'Times up!'

'What five bloody seconds. No wait, is it one of his history plays?'

'Each clue will cost you one more breakfast duty. No it isn't a history play'

'No, but you're talking about an inheritance?'

'Mmm'

'So it has to contain a monarch or a Duke or someone like that'

'Getting warm' and he slipped his left hand under her left breast.

'Stop distracting me you rotter. Ooh that's nice. No Sam!'

'Give up?'

'Got it!' she shouted.

'If you really have I'll get breakfast all week'

'Promise?'. Sam gave a scouts' honour sign. 'Right - *A Midsummer Night's Dream*' Kate declared triumphantly.

'You're just too good'

'Hey I'm right. Got you Sam Woodhouse'

Kate leaped out of bed and did a sexy dance of exaltation around the room. 'Who gets to lie in Sam? - me, me me!'

'No first you've got to tell me which characters'

'Sorry not part of the deal. Want to try for another week?' Kate taunted.

'I give up you brilliant blonde bombshell. Who are they anyway?'

'Well for Henry read Theseus Duke of Athens and for Mary read Demetrius one of the suitors of Hermia the daughter of Egeus'

'And why Miss Smartypants? or sometimes Nopants' he added with a smile.

Kate now made her voice more superior and lofty 'Because Theseus insists, against Egeus' wish, that Hermia be allowed to marry her true love Lysander who will therefore inherit Egeus' estates and they will not pass to his selection, namely Demetrius.

'Lady you are good'. Sam pecked her cheek. 'So if she recognised the allusion did Queen Elizabeth approve of this exposure of her father's rule-bending?'

'Well, Shakespeare lightened the situation by depicting the act in a farcical comedy but he was making a point. I see that, now that you've drawn a parallel with Mary's dilemma Sam. Do I pass?'

'You do, with honours, and now you can have your prize'

Kate giggled and dived under the duvet.

Chapter Twenty-Seven

Mary's health was not improving and so, after a prolonged long-distance intercourse between her, the Earl of Shrewsbury and Queen Elizabeth, it was eventually agreed that she be allowed to spend some weeks at the nearby spa town of Buxton in order to bathe in the remedial well-waters there. Shrewsbury even built a special house adjacent to the baths, in the interests of security as much as anything, to prevent any escape attempt by the Scottish Queen.

The highlights of her time now were those days on which she received a letter from Will. In his last one he had told her that the company was about to embark on a five week tour of the North of England but "although my darling I will then be unable to receive your letters which keep alight my soul, for I know not exactly where we will be heading and our address will be constantly changing. I will however write to you at Chatsworth". Now Mary's dilemma was that she too was about to be removed for a month and would not therefore be receiving Will's epistles. Furthermore she had no means of informing him that she would be staying at Buxton.

Mary had spent a lonely three weeks in the spa town but her time had been the happier for having met a number of the local people and endearing herself to them as she invariably did to most folk that she encountered.

One afternoon she was bathing with a group of these ladies, who had now become acquaintances through regular contact. As she entered the waters they were agitatedly talking of a major event which was to occur at the weekend. Mary was preparing to listen to their explanation for the excitement when a rich and sonorous voice rang out from beyond the wall dividing the women bathers from the males. 'Come boys 'tis time we left. Much longer in this water and I will be a pickled herring'.

The women looked at each other, unused to hearing any noise from their hidden fellow bathers.

The man continued 'Six, seven, eight. We are one short. Oh God it is the miserable one again' and the volume increased as he boomed out 'Wherefore art thou Shakespeare?'

Mary froze.

Moments later the voice she loved called back 'I come Walter'.

The Queen of Scots stunned not only the female townsfolk but also the Marys Seton and Livingstone as she screamed out 'Will!' and after a five second pause seeming to last ten minutes she heard a response

'Marie! Marie it cannot be!'

Total silence now reigned amongst the ladies as Mary, as regally as possible for one in a rushing panic, made her way back to the robing rooms. From over the wall came the sound of frantic splashing.

In the foyer of the Baths a wet-haired couple ran to each other and locked themselves into a silent hug that appeared to be eternal to surprised onlookers. A muffled voice against the lad's shoulder cried 'Mon cheri, mon cheri. My Will, my love' and the youth was seen to stroke his fingers through the shining tawny locks of the older woman's hair before both of them burst out crying, still fast together.

The watchers moved on and the lovers were alone. They walked-hand in-hand to a secluded corner. Will looked into Mary's face and lightly brushed away her tears. 'Marie! I have no words, I am lost for them' and they locked lips again.

When language returned to Shakespeare he asked 'But how Marie? What strange reason brings you here?'

'Darling Will I have the same question for you. I have come here to improve my health which has been poor since leaving Bolton Castle. It has been agreed by Elizabeth and Shrewsbury that I may take the waters here for one month before returning to Chatsworth House. Oh Will I could not write to tell you and have received no letters since I left there three weeks ago. But my lover how has this miracle occurred? Tell me what brought you to Buxton'

'In truth my dear the horse-drawn cart' he joked, his whole demeanour now transformed by seeing his queen. 'Did you receive my news that I was leaving to take our plays around the North? '. Mary smiled and nodded her head. 'Well we have been on the road, as my fellows term it, for almost four weeks and are on our way back to Lancashire. This coming Saturday afternoon and evening we are giving performances in the Council Chambers here in Buxton. It will be rewarding to act for a more public audience than those we have been playing to in homes of the aristocracy'

'So you are staying nearby until Sunday?'

'Aye we are that my royal lass'. Mary giggled for the first time in many months. 'We are camped out on the road to Macclesfield'.

The Queen of Scots slowly draped her arms around Shakespeare's neck and put her face close to his 'And shall I see you again Will? For I cannot lose you yet'

'Marie of course. But where do you reside?'

'In the new house just next to these baths, one hundred steps from here'

'In that case there must surely be a way, for I feel a rheumatic ache coming into my limbs and must most certainly take the waters each day'.

Mary had that self-satisfied smirk on her face and Will knew that his words were about to be twisted back at him. 'And sir you have in fact told me before of a limb which aches for me have you not?' and she slid her hand between their bodies to sense the reaction to her words and kisses, mumbling 'Oh Will I had all but forgot this feeling'. As they separated their lips Mary's voice was excited 'My man I have it! '. Will looked amazed. 'Is Fulke with you in Buxton?' she asked almost frantically, her eyes bulging.

'Why yes but he did not care to come with us to the Baths'

'Then Will, tomorrow you must bid him come here and tell him to carry by secret means some items of your apparel. Do you share a wagon with him?'

'Just the two of us'. Mary burst out laughing. 'What is it Marie?'

'I know that Marie Seton has never lain with a man, nor even ever slept in the same room as one, but tomorrow night, and hopefully on Saturday too, she shall share a wagon with Gyllom'. She chuckled again.

'And I will…..'

'Exactly, you will make a fine Marie young sir'

They hugged before wandering out into the gardens of the Baths.

'Are you not accompanied here Marie?'

'Certain sure I am, by two of my Maries and by Swain, but he will not be expecting me to emerge from the waters until four o'clock'. Mary's mood was light now for she had rediscovered herself. 'Will have you never thought it strange that my four companions since childhood all bear the name Marie?'

'Indeed I've always thought it a quirk'

'Even moreso when one learns that in France a maidservant is termed a *marie*; so I thereby have four Maries as *maries*.' The queen smiled as she suggested 'And I am Mister Shakespeare's marie and he my master'

'I think my lady Marie that no man has ever been nor will be your master' and her throaty laugh was music to Will's ears.

'I would that we could be together this night Will but at least we know we have tomorrow. I shall come to the Baths at two o'clock of the afternoon. May we meet outside the robing-rooms at half-past three, there to effect our 'sexchanges'?' My darling Will I must now return to await my jailer's man. Until tomorrow mon precieux garcon'

'Garcon, a boy?'

'Oui one with the powers of a man in youthful form'

'And soon to be a maid'.

They kissed under the pear-tree. 'Dearest Will I hate to see you go'

'Marie my darling woman, it gives me a sour taste to leave you, yet our parting is a sweet sorrow for this is a wondrous day that we have met and now I bid goodbye until the morrow' and as he spoke Shakespeare raised his right arm dramatically in a deliberately exaggerated act of melodrama.

'Oh William such poetry' she laughed –'You should write that down and save it for one of your playlets that you hope to write'.

Fulke was overjoyed to hear that Will had rediscovered his amour, 'Perhaps now Shakespeare we will see a different countenance for surely your face has long been carrying but one expression, that of a doomed tragedian.

'I grant you my moods have been limited Gyllom'

'Moods? No plurals sir, you cannot multiply your state of these past months. Whatever. So this Miss Seton, will she expect me to bed her Will?'

'I think Fulke that if such a thought had entered her head she would now be on a boat to France' he laughed.

The gender-swaps went smoothly and as each party exited their seemingly inappropriate robing-room Will passed on some thespian tips to Mistress Seton: 'Ma'am I would say that nine tenths of a physical portrayal is in the walk. To appear older one walks flat on the heels with shorter strides, but you must step out boldly as a young man'

'So you are bold sir?' interceded Will's Marie, 'Yes I give you that' she conceded after a false consideration. 'And Will I must tell you that when I speak with my Maries it is always in French, so when we are in company you should merely answer me with an occasional 'oui' or 'non' or any other vocabulary that you possess'

'I know of 'chere', 'cherie', and yes 'precieuse' he flippantly offered, receiving a reproving glance from Mary before she kissed him, causing her female companion to study the sky and Fulke to gaze in envy.

'Oh I now see my maidservant in a different light' she joked, stroking his gown fondly. The other pair slipped silently away

'Not merely a reversal of gender but also one of roles eh Will, for certainly I have never before undressed my maid' and Mary gave out one of her delightful giggles as, in the privacy of her bed-chamber, she began to unlace the back of Will's dress. His expression was an incongruous mix of embarrassment at this moment together with excitement at those to follow. His lover knelt down to pull the heavy gown from his waist 'Mais quel surprise!' and she feigned shock as she put one hand to her forehead and the other in Will's groin. She stood up and offered her back to him 'And now my marie you may perform your nightly duty'

'Would that it were as regular' said Will emphatically as he slid his hands round inside her camisole to cup those breasts that he had thought of agonisingly every night.

'Oh Will that feels so good but make haste mon cher for I want you' and Mary helped him to finish her disrobing before grabbing his hand and pulling him to the bed.

As they lay gently stroking in their afterglow Mary pointed out 'Will no-one can say our love life is unvaried for you have taken me to bed dressed as a boy and now I you clothed as a woman' and again Shakespeare heard her sexy titter of amusement before they took each other in their arms, to revel again in the glory of the bodies that they had been missing so desperately.

It had been agreed that Fulke would escort Mary Seton back to the gates of Queen Mary's residence at ten o'clock the next morning, there to effect the re-transformations of her and his friend, but at this hour the two lovers had just drifted off to sleep again.

Mary Livingstone had to think quickly for she had seen Gyllom and her colleague waiting outside but if they hovered there much longer then their guardian Swain would become suspicious as to why two male youths were watching the house. She took the initiative and wandered down to the gates with one of Mary Seton's dresses smuggled under her own skirts. Fulke and Miss Seton were surprised to see her but without questioning they obeyed her instructions to make their way round to the boundary wall skirting the back garden where she would throw over the dress for her colleague.

This accomplished Fulke threw back Will's attire before giving the real marie a lift onto the top of the wall and poor Mistress Seton had to throw herself down into a rhododendron bush. The two women called over to Fulke, telling him to return to his encampment and Will would join him there 'when he and our mistress have completed their business'.

'I bid you farewell ladies but could you please remind Mister Shakespeare that we are giving a matinee performance at two o'clock this afternoon'. He parted with an amused smile and a resigned shake of the head.

At one o'clock the boom of the town cannon, announcing that in one hour's time the play would commence, was sufficient to waken Will and Mary with a start.

'Oh Marie the play! But I have the vestments of a woman and must hurry to the Council Chambers at once'. Right on cue Mary Livingstone, who had been living up to her title as a lady-in-waiting outside the door for two hours, knocked and entered bearing the pile of Shakespeare's clothes.

'Fear not Will, as you see my maries do resolve all problems' Mary reassured him...

As soon as the patient maid had left Will began jumping into his clothes, at the same time hurriedly throwing words at Mary 'Oh Marie what have we done? I fear I will be in trouble with my new employers? My darling I will see you tonight yes?'

'Yes, yes mon cher. We will meet at my gates at eleven o'clock, where we should have been some three hours since if you had not detained me in this bed'. Will loved that dimpling at the corners of her mouth.

'But can you not come to the performance this evening?'

'I can ask Shrewsbury but Will I hold little hope'.

Shakespeare looked quickly around the room whilst straightening his attire.

'Come kiss me Will' and Mary threw back the covers and opened her arms and legs.

'Madam if I come to you like that they will be an actor short this afternoon'

'Then I shall come to you' and Mary exaggerated her sinuous walk as she brought her naked body up against him.

Now even more flustered Will gave her one long kiss then dashed from the room to the sound of his woman's laughter.

Chapter Twenty-Eight

Sam woke up feeling Kate's lips brushing his. Her face looked serious. 'Kate?' he queried,

'Yes of course it's Kate' she laughed, 'It's me on Thursdays remember?'

'That's better' Sam smiled back relievedly, 'You looked so worried though'

'Not really. It's just that I've been awake since seven, thinking. Sam I'm going back to England. Sod the 'financial implications' as the greysuits call them. Both of us are wasting valuable time here. If anywhere we should be in Scotland not bloody Italy'

'You sure?'

'Sure I'm sure. I mean look, tomorrow we're off to Venice for a few days. Great we'll enjoy it, as tourists and you know Venice well anyway so we can have a good time, but it's bugger-all to do with Shakespeare'.

'*Merchant of Venice? Othello?*' proffered Sam.

'Yes right. Merchant of Venice, a play set in Venice and you never hear the word 'water'. The place is a liquid maze and... It might as well be titled 'The Merchant of Manchester' - lots of Jews there - and a canal actually'

'Never thought of it like that'

'Yes well. Anyway you're not getting anywhere with your stuff whilst you're over here Sam. I mean it's been fantastic being here with you, lots of great, what did you call them? grockle-sights etcetera, and brilliant shagging, but why don't we go home?'

'If you're O.K. with that Kate I agree but I don't want it to mess up your Ph.D.'

'I'll phone up my tutor today and explain that Italy is irrelevant to the new direction of my thesis and get him to clear it with the Admin Office for me to return to the UK. I'll be giving them grant-money back, they should be glad. Oh let's forget it for now. Do we have breakfast before or after you get the boiled eggs Samuel?'.

He pulled her to him, delaying his culinary duties until mid-morning.

Venice never failed to thrill Sam. He loved to try and get lost amongst the labyrinth of tiny alleyways, away from the hordes of umbrella-following tourists in St. Mark's Square.

To give Kate an immediate feel of the unique way of life of the Venetians, as they walked down the steps from the station Sam led her to a little jetty where for one euro each they boarded one of the ferry-gondolas, a *traghetto,* which carried them across the Grand Canal to near Piazza Roma. Amongst the group of office-workers they did not wish to appear to be obvious tourists so, like the locals, they remained standing in the narrow vessel, clenching their knuckles as the boat rocked on the wash from a huge vegetable-carrying barge which passed across their bows. Fifty yards away they boarded a number one *vaporetto* water-bus for the ride down the most famous waterway in the world, calling at numerous floating stops to collect passengers from each side of the Grand Canal. They passed the unique waterfront buildings, once splendid palaces, most of which now displayed an air of decayed grandeur. Disembarking at the stop before St. Mark's Square they transferred to a number two waterbus which Sam explained would take them along the not so well-known *Rio Nuovo* canal into the heart of real Venice. On this 'second-division canal' as Sam put it they passed under a series of tiny stone footbridges criss-crossing this fairyland city and saw aquatic versions of usual urban places, like the fire-station containing red and white gondolas and motor-boats. Staying on the vaporetto they completed the circle back to St. Mark's before getting off and wandering past the Doge's Palace and the Campanile bell-tower. Kate was mystified by the groups of Germans, Americans and Japanese sitting at the tables of the two rival cafes on each side of the square where the provision of a small live orchestra apparently justifies them paying ten pounds for a cappuccino.

In a side street only minutes away Sam and Kate ate anti-pasta followed by tortellini and portions of tiramisu which were fit to feed the gods. 'And all for the price of a coffee with music' she pointed out.

It was now siesta time and the lanes were deserted as they meandered past intriguing little shops, some of which ignored siesta closing-time to catch the mad dogs and Englishmen.

'Oh Sam I must buy a mask, aren't they incredible?'

'Yes good idea, like you need to cover up that gorgeous face of yours I don't think'

'Smoothie!' she smiled and stuck two fingers in her mouth. The owner kept her distance as they inspected her wares. 'Sam look at this horrible one, it's got a nose that's almost as long as your...'. Kate was interrupted by the proprietress loudly clearing her throat before informing them quietly that 'I 'ave to speak the good Eenglish signorina'. Kate acknowledged the owner's admission and grinned half-embarrassedly at Sam who decided to re-tie his shoelaces.

'We 'ave beeger noses over 'ere signorina'

'No, I don't want to make you feel inferior' Kate whispered to Sam. The woman did not hear. Kate bought a beautiful shiny black porcelain mask with gold lips and two hearts painted on the left cheek'

'*Che romantica signorina, questa e bellissima* like you. I see you two are very much in lurve I theenk' and she kissed each of them in turn.

As they left Kate turned to Sam 'What a lovely lady. I feel as if we have been blessed by her'. Sam's eyes were leaking.

Kate and Sam sat sipping their glasses of Valpolicella on the little balcony overlooking the narrow side-water canal running alongside their hotel. As the sun sank lower they were listening to the rhythmic slapping of the water against the walls when Kate broke the silence 'Sam I'm really more and more intrigued by your Mary, she must have had immense character'

'She certainly had. A brilliant sense of humour too, very ironic at times. I read that even after she had been sentenced to death, after a ridiculous stitch-up trial, which incidentally was totally illegal because as Mary pointed out, and Elizabeth knew too, a monarch can only be tried by an equal and therefore the whole process was against English Common Law, unless Liz turned up as a judge!. Mary wasn't even allowed counsel but defended herself and was clever enough to tie the lawyers up in knots. Of course the result was a foregone conclusion anyway. Where was I? Oh yes, sense of humour. Yes as she was leaving the courtroom she smiled at the table of prosecution lawyers and said "May God keep me from having to deal with you all again".'

'Now that is cool!' said Kate admiringly. 'But Sam where did she go after Bolton Castle?'

'She was moved to Tutbury Castle on the Staffordshire/ Derbyshire border, apparently a terribly dilapidated place even then. I visited the ruins last year. The sixth Earl of Shrewsbury was her jailer, for fifteen years I think, and she kept being moved around between various of his houses; Chatsworth, Tixall, Wingfield'.

'So do you think, do we think, that she and Shakespeare carried on their love affair?'

'I don't know sweetheart. I'd like to think so. She was executed in February 1587 so Will would have been only twenty-two then, but he had married Anne Hathaway'

'Yes but at the Conference I heard that Shakespeare didn't always remain at Stratford even after their first kid was born. He used to go off touring with Lord Strange's Men; they were the acting company of the fourth Earl of Derby's son - the earl that Will went to after Lord Hesketh I believe'

'So maybe he did keep in touch with Mary on his travels with them'

'Oh I hope so Sam. It's like they were a parallel couple to us in a way. Quite romantic!'

'You're going gooey on me Kate'

'Hey what do you think Mary and Will did after a good drink of wine?'

'Oh-oh!'

'Exactly' and she took his hand and led him slowly back into their room.

The next morning they took the ferry across the Lagoon to the island of Burano, a beautiful unspoilt place, a mini-Venice with its own network of canals but instead of ostentatious palaces the waterways were lined with tiny cottages painted in a variety of pastel colours. There was a great sense of spaciousness and the century could have been any of the last five or six. Old ladies sat in the sunshine outside their homes making lace, the product for which Burano is famous.

Sam followed Kate into a small shop where she picked up a large circular place-mat with a hole at its centre. She led him behind a cane partition and slipped it over her head and ruffled it up 'Voila - Queen Mary!'

Sam laughed, 'Right I'm buying that for you' and with it still around her neck he dragged her to the till where the gnome-like old lady betrayed not the slightest sign of amusement as these crazy foreigners paid for her piece of work.

They found a shady corner of a piazza and sat outside the bar drinking italian beers. Sam looked seriously at Kate 'I think we will last won't we?'

'Only forever Sam' and she gave him a gentle but lengthy kiss. 'Of course we will man, we're chemically bonded'

'Now you're getting sentimental' he mocked. 'Love you lass'

'I love you fella.

They could not get a flight back from Verona for four days so the next morning they took the coach to Venice's Marco Polo Airport and flew home from there, now seeming just another couple of holidaymakers - Kate's return journey being so different from her feeling of desolation on the flight to Italy.

'Worthwhile coming out here?' Sam asked her

'Well it would have been but my studies got interrupted by this horny historian'. The hand that she was sitting on clenched her bottom, provoking a head-turning squeal – the English passengers deciding that a father was obviously teasing his daughter whereas the Italians enjoyed this play between a pair of lovers.

Chapter Twenty-Nine

Mary was granted permission by the Earl of Shrewsbury to attend the evening performance of the play but this was then withdrawn at five o'clock. The reason, unbeknown to Mary, was that the Earl had had his mind changed for him by the surprise visitor who arrived that afternoon - Sir Francis Walsingham, Queen Elizabeth's much-feared henchman, her spymaster. Had Mary known of his presence then she would have been frightened of attempting a second Fulke-Mary Seton exchange, which nevertheless went smoothly as arranged later that night.

Sir Francis had made the journey north because for several months word had been reaching Elizabeth that Mary Queen of Scots was virtually holding court in the Midlands, despite her supposed imprisonment. Certainly a succession of influential callers at Tutbury and Chatsworth could have given cause for alarm to the English Queen. Sir William Cecil's envoy to Ireland, Nicholas White, wrote to his master after calling at Tutbury on his way to Ireland. Whilst claiming that he was immune to the charms of Mary he admitted that "She hath withal an alluring grace, a pretty accent, and a searching wit, clouded with mildness".

Walsingham had come to demand that Shrewsbury's control of the Scottish Queen be tightened, with further restrictions on her freedom of movement outside of her domiciles. She was no longer to be permitted to go hunting and even trips into the countryside to practice her sporting passion for archery were to cease.

On the Sunday morning, after a completely sleepless night spent by the two ardent lovers, Mary informed her guard that the man with her would be joining them '...to practice with my bow and arrows'. Word of the restrictions had not yet filtered down to him. Will was introduced as 'The son of a former friend of mine, an accomplished carpenter who has come to solve a problem with my bed..'. The guard did not hear Mary's whispered aside to Will as she squeezed his hand '...for it is too lonely'.

The Earl's servant was bored by his inactive duty and soon dozed off under an oak tree, missing the lovers' pranks as they took breaks from their archery. Mary pulled open her bodice to bare her breasts 'You see Will here is the scar from where your arrow entered my heart at Bolton Castle'. Shakespeare peered playfully but could not spot a mark and therefore had to inspect at the closest quarters until Mary laughingly pulled his mouth to her nipple.

The couple were still light-heartedly exchanging banter when they re-entered the gates of her latest prison. As the guard walked away carrying the equipment Mary and Will turned to walk between the high box-hedges of the garden. They suddenly heard a jangling noise behind them and their mood changed, taking a dramatic dive when they saw before them two more guards and the gaunt figure of Sir Francis Walsingham. Will wrapped his arm around Mary but it was wrenched away from her by one of the men behind them. Both his arms were then locked up behind his back as he was pushed forward to face Walsingham.

'I believe you to be William Shakespeare of Stratford-upon-Avon, formerly in the employ of that Catholic fiend Sir Alexander Hoghton and thereafter in service under his friend Sir Thomas Hesketh. Do you identify yourself so?'

'What is the meaning of this?'. Mary had lost none of her authoritarial tone. 'Who are you sir?'

'Sir Francis Walsingham ma'am, at your service' he sneered. Mary's gasp was involuntary. She had finally met the man that Catholics saw as the most hated man in England. She crossed herself.

'Answer me. Are you Shakespeare?'

'I am'

'The same Shakespeare who endeavoured to assist this woman to escape from Hoghton Tower?'

Will had no chance to reply before his beloved Mary again interceded on his behalf, her bravado now restored as she commanded 'Walsingham you serpent, take us to Shrewsbury'. Surprisingly the grim-faced captor conceded to her demand and Will was forcefully ushered into the house.

'Shakespeare you were warned at Hoghton Tower yet still you associate with Mary Queen of Scots. I have spoken with the Earl of Shrewsbury and he now understands that she is to be restrained from associating with people suspected of Roman Catholic sympathies. This includes you. Should you ever again attempt to visit this woman there will be no further pardons, you will be taken into the Tower of London where you will be charged with treason against Her Majesty Queen Elizabeth. The sentence for this act I am sure you know'. With that Walsingham moved to leave but paused and turned at the doorway, 'Master Shakespeare I order you to leave these premises with me'. He nodded to two of his men waiting outside the open door. They collected Will and dragged him to the gates. Mary accompanied him and ignored the spy's damnations as she kissed Will goodbye.

Will had been returned to his companions by Walsingham's men that afternoon but now, under cover of darkness, and ignoring Fulke's exhortations to 'stop thinking with your pistol!' he had returned in an attempt to see Mary again before the players moved on the following morning. Three times Shakespeare attempted to climb the ivy-cladding beneath the balcony to Mary's room. Finally he managed it and clambered over the balustrade. The curtains were still open and a candle burnt in the room. Will carefully looked through the french-windows and eventually saw Mary walk across her room. He could tell from her actions that she was alone and he tapped the glass. Her head shot round, looking shocked, then she saw her man and a smile burst from her lips and eyes. She hurried to undo the doors. 'Oh mon cheri, my darling Will. But you are crazy!'

'Mad for you my love' and they hugged each other tightly.

'Dear Will I fear for your life. Walsingham was not joking when he spoke of The Tower'

'Marie I could not leave you in that way, being dragged from you'

'Will I was preparing for my bed, dreading a night lying awake thinking of you'

'Then let nothing change ma cherie, for I will surely be lying in your bed thinking of you this night'. Mary beamed as he began to unlace her gown.

It was in the early hours of the morning when Mary and Will, gasping from their ardours, heard a crash as the door burst open and there stood Walsingham. Mary screamed and Will grasped her to him, seeking to protect her rather than dash for the balcony.

'Take him!'

Will gave Mary a kiss which lasted until he was thrown to the floor.

'Put on your garments traitor' snapped the intruder. Will's wrists were bound tightly behind his back and he turned to his lover as he was bundled to the door. Her tears were flooding but she managed to blow him a loving kiss.

Chapter Thirty

Sam and Kate lived for most of the time at her cottage but sometimes for a break they would go over to Barnard Castle to stay at Sam's place, walking on the Pennines where the air was so 'bracing' as Sam called it on one occasion when they were able to body-surf into a gale blowing on the top of Bowes Moor.

One day in 'Barnie' Sam bought from a second-hand bookshop a battered paperback copy of a book by Edith Sitwell, *The Queens and the Hive*, telling of the rival lives of Mary and Elizabeth. He sat engrossed in it all evening, not even Kate's naked cartwheels could distract him from it. She eventually resorted to climbing over the back of his chair and sliding down head-first between him and the book.

'Is my appeal waning Sam?' she giggled, knowing full well that there was not the remotest possibility of that occurring.

Sam gently patted the bare bottom in front of his face as he spoke, 'I've found something amazing here, I'll tell you if you get yourself upright madam'

'Like you seem to be doing from where I am' she tittered

'Kate this could be dynamite'.

She slid down to sit at his feet, 'Tell me oh wise one, or is it old wise one?' she teased, as she lay her head in his groin and looked up into his face. 'Tell me Sam please'

'Ok,. page 340, and here the author is writing about Mary's time under the Earl of Shrewsbury. You ready?'

'Ready Samuel'

'Right. "An innkeeper of Islington, named Walmesley, was in the habit of telling his guests that the Earl of Shrewsbury had gotten the Scottish Queen with child, and that he knew where the child was christened".'

'Holy shit!'

'As you say, but...'

'No let me say it Sam'. He smiled benevolently then tweaked her left breast

'You sod! Right, my idea is...' and she grinned cheekily, '...what if Mary did have a baby and, knowing what we know - it wasn't the Earl's but...' and Kate leapt up in the air with arms and legs splayed '...it was fucking Shakespeare's!'

'My thoughts exactly young lady but perhaps not so colourfully expressed' and Sam's pseudo-professorial tone was the perfect complement. Kate threw herself in a ball onto his lap.

'Sam what if it were true? Just imagine what a child that would have been, mixing the genes of Mary and Will. Wow!'

'I guess we will never know sweetheart'

'I love that word, I have done since you first called me that'

'Kiss me Kate'

She did.

'Kiss me Sam'

He did.

'Marry me Kate'

'Marry me Sam'

They agreed.

The wedding date was fixed, romantically and perhaps a little morbidly, for February 8th, the anniversary of Mary's execution. Kate wanted the ceremony to be held near to where they had first met so they booked it at the Registrar's office in Leyburn, with the reception at 'The Golden Lion' hotel. 'It's where we first had sex' Kate freely admitted to the handful of friends that they invited, giving such information on the bottom of the cards she sent out.

Kate came back from university one afternoon feeling quite weary after a lengthy session with her supervisory tutor. Sam's news though caused her spirits to soar.

'You haven't!' Her eyebrows rose skywards.

'What did I promise you that day we went back to look at it?'

'That we would one day end up sleeping in Mary's bed. But how? You didn't tell me either you devil!'

'No' he laughed, 'I've been waiting for the Honourable Harry to reply. I'd written and explained who we are and where we wanted to spend our honeymoon night. He was brilliant. He phoned me this morning. He remembered us. In fact he pointed out that he was actually there when I promised you'

'Yes that's right'

'Anyway he thinks it's a great idea and he's promised to air the bedding for us when it gets near the time'

'Oh Sam I wish it was now'

'Won't be long my precious. Do you think we should abstain from sex until the wedding day?'

'Oh yes, definitely. Good idea', but Kate was unzipping his jeans as she spoke.

Chapter Thirty-One

Shakespeare was incarcerated in The Tower for three terrible weeks, the conditions there being beyond the imagination of any humane soul.

Then one day the door to his tiny low-ceilinged cell was opened and he was pulled out by his ankles to look up at the faces of Sir Francis Walsingham and Ferdinando, Lord Strange, the son of the Earl of Derby. Will was taken upstairs.

Walsingham began in his usual stern tone 'William Shakespeare I believe you know Lord Strange, the son of your former employer. Unlike his father he has sworn loyalty to Queen Elizabeth and the Protestant cause'. Will saw that Ferdinando bore that superciliously pious look of the newly-converted. Walsingham continued 'The Earl of Derby's Players are to be no more; they are to become Lord Strange's Men. You will join them...' Will inwardly sighed with relief at this apparent reprieve from execution. '...where you will convince your new master that you are no longer a Roman Catholic. Do you understand?' Will gave a reluctant nod. 'Do you understand sir!' he bellowed.

'Yes' Shakespeare replied, without enthusiasm.

'I further understand from Lord Strange that you have shown some promise as a poet and a writer of playlets. I should warn you that all such writings in England today are to be in support of the Protestant religion, with condemnation of Rome where possible'. Will looked up at these words, never having given consideration to censorship of his work. Walsingham continued, offering Shakespeare a carrot, 'Should you further your playwriting career, and should it show promise, then you could one day have the opportunity to serve our glorious Queen Elizabeth'. Will remained silent, as he had been instructed to do. 'Do you hear me Shakespeare?'

'I hear you Sir Francis'

'Take him away and scrub him'. Then he turned to Lord Strange 'Then sir he is yours'. Walsingham spun on his heel and left.

Will saw Queen Elizabeth's spymaster one more time before leaving with Lord Strange. Walsingham walked up to Will, put his face close to his and spoke with venom in his voice 'Your royal mistress no longer sends or receives letters Shakespeare and should you ever again attempt to see her there will be no more reprieves'. The man's icy calm cracked as he slapped his glove across Will's face.

It was many years later, some time after the execution of the love of his life, that Shakespeare again visited the Tower of London. This time he was to play before the Governor as one of the leading lights of the Lord Chamberlain's Men, the professional acting company appointed by Queen Elizabeth and founded largely from Lord Strange's Men.

As they dined after the performance a stooped ancient-looking fellow approached Will, tapped him on the shoulder and furtively handed him a piece of dusty parchment. Will left the table and found a secluded corner. His whole body tensed up as he recognised the handwriting on the outside of the document. It was addressed to "Will Shakespeare, Another Imprisoned Wrongfully, The Tower of London ". Hands shaking Will untied the faded ribbon and read:

"Mon cheri, ma vie

If music be the food of love
Dear Will
I am starving from the silence
And fear to live I've lost
My will.

Marie"

Chapter Thirty-Two

The wedding was a splendid occasion. Despite the mundane locale of the service the bride and groom were determined to get married with style. Kate's dress was a beautifully rustic creation, in pale green, of a shepherdess' gown with a matching head-dress tied by a silk rope. Sam had been asked by her to choose between a kilt, in deference to their Scottish queen or Shakespearean doublet and hose and despite Kate's revelling in his trying on of the tights he opted for the kilt, 'But no groping during the ceremony you!' he had ordered her. His Celtic attire was matched by the tartan mini-skirt worn by Jessie the Glaswegian chambermaid who they had invited to the wedding.

'Well Sam she was the first person in the world to see us together' Kate had reminded him. Today though the girl's hair was of a magnificent multi-coloured Stewart plaid design,

'Och when I heard as you were fans of oor Queen I cudna resist it' she laughed as she kissed both of them.'

The guests had all been booked into the hotel overnight so they merely had to make their way upstairs after the reception whereas the newlyweds were collected by a taxi which carried them out to Bolton Castle.

They were met at the entrance arch by an aristocratic looking man who introduced himself as Charlie Fotheringham, 'I'm afraid Harry and his wife have had to go to Paris for the week but I think we've organised everything for you. There is a fire in your room so you won't feel cold if you should wake up in the night'. Kate did not appreciate his leering wink.

Left alone the lovers looked at each other and Kate took Sam's face between her hands, 'Sam, my precious Sam, it seems no time since we met here but we've come a long way fella'. He was too choked by her words to answer. They turned to the bed. 'I always believed you meant it on that first day when you promised me we'd sleep in this. I just felt we were completely matched'

'Me too Queen Kate'

'Sam do you think we have to be careful, you know, I mean its a very old and unique piece of furniture'

'Aren't we always cautious?'.

Kate laughed loud at his outrageous claim.

They undressed each other lingeringly then as they walked towards the historical bed Kate wrapped her arm round Sam's waist and sounded a little wary as she asked him 'Sam isn't this a bit spooky though?'

'Do you wish we weren't spending tonight here darling? We can always go back to the hotel'

'No, I'm just being silly. You can't believe in ghosts can you?'

'That's the spirit!' and Sam's poor pun at least caused them both to laugh as they clambered into the four-poster. The first time they made love it was in fact gently, not for the bed's sake but because such was their mood.

An hour later they were both panting furiously after more frantic lovemaking. They lay with their faces pressed cheek to cheek. The embers of the fire which had been lit for their benefit still cast a light over the room. Suddenly they both tensed up, for there, on the opposite wall, was a huge shadow moving across the room. It stopped and Sam and Kate could discern that it was of human form. The person, whoever it was, reached up to its head and pulled off a nightcap, releasing a cascade of hair. Neither Kate nor Sam spoke. The shadow continued across the wall in their direction and in a French accent asked 'Are you awake?' The figure became clear. Standing there with her red hair haloed by the firelight, was Mary Queen of Scots.

When the actor playing Shakespeare reached his fellow thespian from the Hawes Amateur Players he expected to make up a four-way celebration of Charlie Fotheringham's little joke with Sam and Kate. Instead he found the actress who had played Mary was in the ante-chamber shrieking and crying. He calmed her then she silently took his arm as if dumbstruck. She led him back into the room, he could feel her trembling as she led him to the bed of the newly-weds. 'Mary' pointed down at the couple. Four eyes were staring fixedly into space and were set in rigid gape-mouthed faces which were ashen-white, drained of blood, looking for all the world like two severed heads.